NEAL SHUSTERMAN'S
DARKNESS CREEPING

tales to trouble your sleep

Illustrated by Michael Coy

Lowell House
Juvenile
Los Angeles

CONTEMPORARY
BOOKS
Chicago

OTHER BOOKS BY NEAL SHUSTERMAN

The Shadow Club

The Eyes of Kid Midas

What Daddy Did

Speeding Bullet

Dissidents

Kid Heroes

Designer: Lisa-Theresa Lenthall

Manufactured in the United States of America

ISBN: 1-56565-069-7

Library of Congress Catalog Card Number: 93-13792

10 9 8 7 6 5 4 3 2

For Nolan . . . who likes his stories scary
—N. S.

At the back of your mind, there's a hole open wide,
Where the darkness is creeping in from the outside,
You can light rows of candles to cast the dark out,
But it's always there hiding . . .

. . . in shadows of doubt.

CONTENTS

MONKEYS TONIGHT

MY SISTER WAKES UP SCREAMING AT THE TOP OF HER lungs—a sharp, shrill sound, like an alarm, or a teakettle boiling to death. The awful noise rips me out of the deepest of sleeps. I twist through space until I feel the blanket around me and the coldness of my feet. She screams again, and I pull the blanket over my head, trying to cram it into my ears.

Then I hear the panicked footsteps of my parents as they race down the hall. I glance at the clock. It's almost four in the morning.

Mom and Dad bound into the room as Melinda empties her lungs again, even louder than before.

"Shut her up!" I croak to my parents in a raspy night voice. Mom and Dad ignore me and race to Melinda's bed. They shake her and shake her until she comes out of her nightmare. Her screaming fades into a whimper, but when she sees Mom and Dad above her she begins to sob. Dad takes her into his arms as she cries.

"I'll get her some water," says Mom.

"Bring some for me," I say, knowing that Mom doesn't hear me. She never hears me when Smellinda is crying. Smellinda: that's what I call her, because as far as I'm concerned, she stinks.

"Can't you shut her up?" I plead, trying to stretch the blanket over my freezing feet.

"Ryan, just go back to sleep," says Dad.

Easy for him to say. He doesn't have to share a room with a human air-raid siren. There is something wrong when a twelve-year-old boy is forced to share a room with his eight-year-old sister. There ought to be a law against it.

Dad picks up Melinda and rocks her gently. "What is it, honey?" he asks.

"Monkeys," whimpers Melinda.

I groan and bury my head in my pillow as Mom brings water for Melinda and nothing for me. Why did I know it was going to be monkeys? It's always monkeys.

Monkeys. Of all the dumb things to be afraid of. I mean, there are plenty of *really* scary things to be afraid of, aren't there? Mummies, and skeletons, and spooky graveyards, and vampires. But personally, it's spiders that freak me out. Sometimes I imagine these big, three-foot-long spiders with hairy black legs the size of human arms. They drink your blood, spiders do. Well, not human blood—fly blood. But I suppose if spiders were big enough, they could go for human blood, too. Just the thought of them makes my skin crawl and my heart start to race. But *monkeys?* Who in their right mind is scared of monkeys?

Smellinda, that's who.

Dad holds her and walks back and forth on Melinda's side of the room, full of dolls and rainbow wallpaper. It's the side of the room my friends make fun of when they come over to visit, as if I had anything to say about it.

"There are no monkeys in here," Dad tells Melinda. "It was just a dream. Just your imagination."

"They came down the chimney," she cries. I start to laugh to myself. A few weeks ago we saw a television show about how they transport zoo animals by plane. One of the animals they showed was a monkey. Ever since then, Melinda is certain that every time a plane flies by, a monkey is going to jump out of the plane like a hairy paratrooper and head straight for our chimney.

"There are no monkeys in the room, sweet cakes," says Mom, flicking on the light, blinding me. "See?"

I roll over and bury my face in the pillow.

"The closet," says my sister.

Dad opens the closet to reveal clothes and a messy pile of toys.

"The bathroom," says Melinda.

Dad steps into the bathroom, peeling back the shower curtain to reveal just a leaky faucet and a bathtub ring.

"The kitchen," insists Melinda.

Dad carries her down the hallway, and I hear him and Mom inspect every inch of our house. Closets, cabinets, the oven, the fireplace—they even check under the furniture.

Finally, ten minutes later, they come back with Melinda happily asleep in Dad's arms, satisfied that the house has been purged of the banana-eating menaces. They gently tuck her in, turn off the light, and go back to bed.

Melinda, her nose stuffy from crying, snores away. Even after her monkey fit, she can sleep. But I'm not so lucky. I can hear everything around me. I hear the awful ticking of her Mickey Mouse clock. I hear the *whap!* as the paper boy throws newspapers on driveways long before the sun comes up. When I open my eyes I see shadows and get spooked. The shadows are like fat spiders, with legs stretching along the walls and floor. Darkness creeping, inch by inch toward my bed. I know that it's only clothes piled in the corner, and stuffed animals on the shelves, and patterns cast by the window blind, but still, I see spiders. Once I've got the spider creeps, I know I won't sleep for the rest of the night, no matter how much I want to.

But there's Melinda across the room, sleeping happily with her dolls and purple ponies and fluffy teddy bears. She sleeps peacefully, probably dreaming of a beautiful fairy-tale castle. And I silently wish for her dream castle to be invaded by baboons.

On the drive to school in the morning, Melinda and I sit in the backseat. Melinda plays with Deep Space Barbie, who has blue hair and green skin. I just sit there like a zombie who didn't get enough sleep. How I wish I could go back to bed!

Mom drives, listening to the news, hoping to hear a traffic report. Instead, we hear a story about the zoo.

Tragedy struck at the Central Zoo yesterday, begins the reporter, *when an angry gorilla apparently broke through its cage, grabbed a man, and ripped off—*

CLICK!

Mom quickly truns off the radio, pretending she didn't hear the reporter.

Melinda looks at me with a face that's turning almost as green as Deep Space Barbie. "Ripped off what?" she asks.

"Probably ripped off his arms," I tell her.

"Ryan!" my mother warns.

"Maybe his head, too. Gorillas are known to do that."

"Mommy, what do you think the gorilla ripped off?" Melinda asks tentatively.

"I think it ripped off his wallet," says Mom, "so it could treat Mrs. Gorilla out to a fancy dinner."

Melinda laughs.

"Maybe got his legs, too," I tell Melinda. "Apes are strong. Monkeys are, too. I'll bet if they wanted to, all the gorillas and baboons and orangutans and chimps could break out of their cages and escape in a matter of minutes. Hey, Mom, how far is the zoo from our house?"

"Never mind that!" says Mom.

I snicker, and in a flash of inspiration, I grab Melinda's Deep Space Barbie. "This is probably how it looked at the zoo yesterday." I insert Barbie hair-first into my mouth and bite off her head.

"Mommmmyyyyyyyy!" screams Melinda.

Mom glares at me in the rear-view mirror. "Ryan, stop it!" she yells.

I spit it out and the little plastic head ricochets off the window and lands in Melinda's lap. She puts the head back on, but she can't stop crying. I, on the other hand, can't stop laughing.

It's a full moon tonight. The kind that brings out the were-wolves—if you believe in that stuff. Our house doesn't get werewolves, though. Tonight, we get something else.

I'm fast asleep when I first hear Melinda. She's not

screaming, she's calling my name. "Ryan," she whispers. I'm dragged feet first out of my dream, and twist through space back into my bed, where I open my eyes and see Melinda looking toward me in the dim blue of the moonlit room. It is four o'clock again. I sigh and wish there were a Sister Fairy who would come in the night to take Melinda away, leaving a quarter beneath my pillow. Fair exchange.

"Ryan," she whispers. "Do you hear that?"

Scrape, scrape, scrape. It could be coming from anywhere.

"It's probably just a stray cat," I tell her. "Go to sleep." But the sound gets louder. *Scrape! Scrape! Scrape!* Now I can hear the hiss and rattle of falling debris.

"It's coming from the chimney!" says Melinda.

"Naah, it's probably just Dad making some weird late-night snack," I say, but now the sound has got me worried, too.

I sit up and listen. There's a noise coming from the hardwood floor in the living room. The squishy sound of barefeet—*plod-plod-plod*—but then the sound is gone. *It's in the hallway,* I tell myself. *It's walking on the carpeted hallway, silently.*

It's much too quiet. I can hear the ticking of the clock pounding in my ears like a woodpecker. I am about to announce to Melinda that it was just her imagination when a shadow leaps into the room, howling.

It's a monkey—laughing in a crazy, screeching, evil voice. I see it, but I don't believe it. I am too shocked to scream.

"Ryan?" Melinda's high-pitched, panicked voice is like a squeaky wheel. "No . . . no," she whines. She tries to scream, but it's like her throat is all closed up in fear. She starts batting the air around her. "Go away! Go away!"

A second monkey runs into the room, jumps up on a shelf, and begins throwing books everywhere.

Another monkey comes in through the window and terrorizes Melinda, flailing its hands in her face and making awful noises. Melinda gasps, unable to catch her breath in fear. Then she screams, and so do I. That's when the room explodes into a mad monkeyhouse. The closet door flies open and they leap out like commandos—not just monkeys, but apes like chimpanzees and orangutans, too. They charge out of the closet as if the closet is a doorway to another world. Small monkeys with long tails and white faces climb out from the dresser drawers and leap from wall to wall. A single gorilla growls in the doorway, making sure we can't get out. Both of us scream and scream. *Where are our parents? Why can't we hear them coming down the hall?*

One baboon with wild, fiery eyes and sharpened teeth smiles and speaks—*he actually speaks!* "Your parents won't wake up," he sneers. "They won't wake up until morning. We won't let them."

I try to help Melinda, but hairy hands grab me and throw me back against the wall. I can only watch as they torment her, tearing apart her stuffed animals, chewing them to bits, shredding her books, leaping across her bed, and swinging wildly through the room. They pull at her arms and tug at her hair as she screams. An orangutan plays her head like the bongo drums. A chimp makes hideous faces at her, and Melinda keeps screaming in terror, until she finally screams herself out. Soon her voice is gone, but her mouth keeps screaming silently. This is her nightmare—but how did it get out of her head? *How?*

Finally the raid ends, and the apes and monkeys begin to leave. Some climb out of the window, others vanish into the closet, some climb into the dresser drawers and disappear, and others race out of the room and scurry up the chimney. I look to Melinda. She is pale. She looks straight ahead, frozen, but does not see.

"Melinda?"

She will not answer me. It's as if she's gone far away and doesn't even hear me.

"Melinda?"

But she won't talk at all. I think she may never talk again.

The last monkey—the baboon with sharpened teeth—looks around at the ruined room, at the night's work. He leaps up to the windowsill to leave, and I say a prayer of thanks that it's all over. But then he turns to me before he disappears into the night. He smiles at me, showing his terrible teeth. I pull my blanket over me, but it won't cover my feet no matter how hard I try.

"Pleasant dreams, Ryan," he rasps in a deep, scratchy voice. Then he says, with an awful wink:

"Tomorrow night, spiders."

BLACK BOX

THE OLD MAN WORE A PLAYFUL SMILE AS HE BECKONED them closer. Karin and her cousin Randy stepped across the yellowing floor of the immense den, deep within their grandfather's ancient house. They were paying their respects to the old man, as their parents had insisted.

On a cherrywood table rested a menagerie of colorful origami animals—a folded-paper zoo. Karin wondered whether her grandfather spent all his time making them or if he had folded the animals to impress her and Randy, the way he used to when they were five.

He always spoke to them in Chinese first, as if his speaking the language would magically make them understand it better. Karin understood a little bit, but she knew that Randy didn't speak a word—he just squirmed and looked annoyed. For his sake she said, "You have to talk English, Grandfather."

"English!" spat their grandfather, then waved his hand as if swatting the thought away. "Ah! You children lose everything. All the old ways, you lose. How can you call yourselves Chinese?"

"We're not Chinese," Randy said defiantly. "We're American."

Karin gave Randy a sharp elbow to the ribs.

"Don't get him mad!" she whispered.

The old man looked at Randy with hardened eyes, and then he laughed. "Yes. American," he chuckled. "Apple pie!" He laughed and laughed, and Karin elbowed Randy again.

"Don't you know not to say things like that to him?" she said. Randy never did learn how to deal with Grandfather. Still, her cousin was right. They *were* both born in America; even their parents were born in America. How much more American could they get?

Grandfather laughed a little too long, and Karin began to feel uncomfortable.

Fiinally, he shook his head and wiped the tears from his eyes. "Yes. American," he sighed. "The old world is gone. My world—gone. Soon nobody will be left to remember."

"I'll remember," offered Karin.

Grandfather smiled. "Sweet girl," he said. "But stupid."

Randy snickered.

"You should not laugh," said Grandfather, wagging an arthritic finger at him. "Next to you, she looks like a genius."

Karin smiled and gave Randy a smarter-than-you look, then she turned back to the old man. He looked very serious for a moment, then he glanced down at the dark cherrywood table and the collection of paper animals. He picked up a paper cat. "This world of new things—you think it is strong like a lion, when in truth it is fragile like paper."

He crumpled the origami cat in his hand and flicked

it with his finger across the room. "There. Destroyed by a single finger."

Then Grandfather let loose a hacking cough that rattled the room so much Karin wondered how his lungs could stand it. When his coughing fit was over, the old man turned to a shelf filled with old knickknacks and pulled down a black box about the size of a shoe box. At first Karin thought it held tissues, but there was no opening on it. Anywhere.

"This is very old," Grandfather said, brushing his fingers across the smooth, ebony surface. "Even older than me. Hard to believe anything is older than me, hah?" And he let out a laugh that sent him into another coughing fit.

Karin and Randy looked at the box.

"What is it?" Karin asked, as Grandfather handed it to her.

"Puzzle box," answered the old man.

Randy grabbed it from her and pawed his fingers all over it, leaving dull fingerprints on the shiny lacquered surface. "There's no way to open it," he said.

Karin grabbed it back from him and examined it again herself. Randy was right—it was solid all the way around!

Grandfather gently took it back from her. He tapped the top twice, then placed three fingers on one side, two on the other, then pressed inward with his thumbs. A panel slid open. Karin was amazed.

"No way!" said Randy, his eyes wide.

"Way," Grandfather said simply. He pressed and prodded different pressure points, deftly and skillfully, as if playing an instrument. The box began to open up with dark, textured surfaces. When Grandfather was done it looked more like a black flower than a box, and in the center of that flower was another, smaller box, even blacker than the first one. It was perfectly square, about two inches wide.

Karin and Randy just stared. "Another puzzle?" asked Karin.

"No," answered Grandfather. "A solution."

Grandfather held the inner box in his hand and placed his fingertips on it. Instantly, the hinged lid opened, revealing a carved jade panel, and in the center of all that sparkling green jade was a bright gold button. Not the kind of button you wear, but the kind of button you press. Tiny Chinese characters were carved into the jade all around the gold button, but Karin couldn't read them.

"Oooh!" said Karin.

"It must be worth big bucks!" said Randy.

"Never mind that," snapped Grandfather. He put the little box down on the table. Randy and Karin couldn't take their eyes off it.

"I want to give this to the right person before I die," Grandfather said. "Your parents and your older brothers and sisters—they are worse than you. They hate the old ways, and the old things. They want to forget them. This is how I know that one of you must get this gift."

"Thanks!" Randy reached out his hand, but Grandfather slapped it away.

"Not so fast." He picked up the little box and handed it to Karin. Her eyes lit up, and she gazed at it as if it were a diamond ring in a jewelry box.

"You are the trustworthy one. Your cousin Randy here, he would trade this for a baseball card, yes?"

"No!" said Randy, but Karin knew that it probably depended on how good the baseball card was.

Grandfather turned his gaze back to Randy. "I bring you here, Randall, so you will always remember the honor you did not receive from me. Someday you will learn to respect old things."

Randy scowled and pouted, and then said under his breath, "I don't want it. It's a girl's thing, anyway." But he knew that it was not.

Karin moved her finger across the rough jade and around the smooth gold button, then her fingertip came across the button and she started to press it. Grandfather gasped and pulled her finger away with his bony hand.

"You must not!" he cried out. "Can't you read?"

"It's in Chinese," she said, looking at the Chinese characters written around the button.

Grandfather sighed.

"This has been in our family for forty-nine generations," he said. "Fifty-one, now that I pass it on to you. It has been our family's task all these years to guard this button with a clear heart, and a clean mind. Show no one. Tell no one. And never, *ever* press it."

"But what does it do?" asked Karin.

Grandfather leaned closer, speaking in a raspy whisper.

"This," he said, "is the button that ends the world."

That evening Karin sat on a lumpy bed in one of the many upstairs bedrooms of her grandfather's huge house. She puzzled over the puzzle box, practicing how it opened and closed. She had only seen her grandfather do it once, but once was all it took for her to memorize it.

Randy, who lay on the floor tossing a ball at the high ceiling, watched in disgust at how easily Karin could now open the box. She had a photographic memory, and she knew that it irritated Randy to no end.

"He gave it to you because you kiss up to him," said Randy.

"He gave it to me because he knows I'll take care of it."

"*And* because you kiss up to him."

Karin closed the puzzle box and practiced opening it again. There was never much to do on these annual family get-togethers. The other cousins were all either much younger or much older than Karin and Randy. The young ones were all asleep in the maze of bedrooms within Grandfather's immense house. All the adults were downstairs, babbling about nothing important. Their jumbled voices drifted up the great staircase and echoed down the winding halls.

"You don't believe any of that stuff about that stupid button, do you?" scoffed Randy, tossing his ball and watching how close he could come to hitting the light in the center of the ceiling.

Karin pulled out the little box from the center of the puzzle box.

"No . . ." she said.

Randy smirked. "You do believe it—I can tell." He tossed the ball again. "You're as loony as he is."

"I believe some of it," said Karin. "You remember last year I showed everyone that genealogy I did?"

"Genie-what?"

"Genealogy—the family tree."

"Oh yeah, that thing."

"Well, our family does trace back to some sort of royalty. I'll bet that this box really *was* passed down from our ancestors."

"And do you believe it could destroy the world?"

Karin flipped open the little box. She regarded the gold button. It seemed so harmless, and yet . . .

"No," she said. "Of course I don't believe it. But it's strange to think that people *did* believe it, maybe for thousands of years."

"You think anyone's ever pressed it?"

"Probably not," said Karin. "They wouldn't press it if they believed in it."

"This is what I think," said Randy. "A thousand years ago, we had this ancient Chinese nerd relative, and one day his friends gave him this box as a practical joke—and that idiot believed the joke."

Karin tilted the little black box in her hand, and the button reflected a pinpoint of light that danced across the peeling wallpaper.

"I'll bet you don't even have the guts to press it," said Randy, and then his ball went a bit too high, hitting the light above him and smashing it. Randy rolled out of the way just as the glass showered down to the warped wooden floor. Karin froze, closing her eyes and gripping the little black box.

In the silence that followed she could hear shouts from downstairs and the sound of feet running down the hallway toward them. Several people were wailing—it seemed a bit much just for some broken glass.

Randy's father appeared at the door first.

"I'm sorry," said Randy in a panic. "I didn't mean it—it was an accident."

But Karin could tell that her uncle wasn't looking at the glass.

"Randy, Karin," he said, not looking at all well. "I'm afraid something terrible has happened. It's your grandfather."

Grandfather's funeral was held just a day later.

It was more convenient that way, since the whole family was already in town for the annual reunion. No one had expected him to die that night, especially the way it happened. He had fallen through a termite-eaten floorboard, right in front of all the relatives. Leave it to Grandfather to make such a dramatic exit from the world.

Karin's mom had cried hysterically for most of that night. She had been talking to him when it happened. "Just like that," she kept telling everybody. "He was talking to me—he was in the middle of a sentence, *in the middle of a word*—and then suddenly he wasn't there. All that was left was a hole!"

To Karin this was more than an accident. Somehow the old man knew his time was coming. It made Karin wonder what else he might have known.

At the funeral, Karin watched as Randy, on the far side of the casket, squirmed away from his parents and came around to her. His mind, like hers, seemed to be less concerned with Grandfather and more concerned with what Grandfather had left behind. Randy began whispering to Karin while an old woman spoke a Chinese eulogy.

"Do you have it?" whispered Randy.

She knew what he was talking about. "Yes."

"Where?"

"It's in my purse. Leave me alone," said Karin.

"Are you carrying it with you everywhere now?"

Karin sighed, and her parents threw Randy an angry look. Randy shut up, for a little while.

When the ceremony was over and everyone was walking back to the cars, Randy pulled Karin off on a detour through a maze of high, black tombstones—a place Karin didn't want to be, but she didn't resist. She didn't want to think or talk about the button anymore, and yet at the same time, she wanted to talk about it more than anything.

"You must be curious," said Randy.

"I thought you didn't believe in the button," Karin said.

"I don't, but I can still be curious about it, can't I?"

Karin reached into her purse and pulled out the little black box. She opened it to reveal the gold button.

Randy stared at it, practically drooling. He wanted that button, and Karin was beginning to wish that their grandfather had given it to him instead.

"I mean, look at it," he said. "It's not attached to anything. If we took it apart, it would probably just be a gold button and a hollow box. Nothing but air inside."

"You are *not* taking it apart," Karin said sternly.

Randy leaned up against the back of a huge black stone and crossed his arms. "So what do you think it's sup-posed to do? You think it's supposed to send off nuclear mis-siles or something?"

"Don't be dumb," said Karin, chalking up another

mark on her list of Stupid Randy Comments. "When this button was made, there were no missiles."

"So then how is it supposed to end the world? Is it supposed to release evil spirits or something? Or send out poisonous gas? How?"

"I don't know," said Karin, and then she smirked. "Why don't you go back to the grave and ask Grandfather?" And then she whispered, "Put your ear close to the ground. He might answer you."

Randy punched Karin in the arm for that, and Karin whacked him back, hard.

"I don't believe in that dumb thing for a second," insisted Randy. "It's not scientific. I don't believe it."

"Well, whether you believe it or not," said Karin, "you don't have to worry about it anymore, because you're never going to see it again."

"Why not?"

"Because I'm putting it away for good, just like our ancestors did. I'm putting it in a safe place where no one will ever find it, until it's my turn to pass it on."

Karin slipped the little box back into her purse, thinking of all the places she could put it where it would be safe until she was about ninety years old. The problem was, she didn't know of such a place.

That night was their last in Grandfather's house. No one wanted to stay there anymore. It wasn't just that he was dead, it was the way the wood creaked when you walked on it—as if it could give way any moment the way it did beneath Grandfather. It was frightening to think that a house so big, which looked so sturdy, could be so fragile.

Karin did not sleep that night—not because of Grandfather's death, and not because of the termite-eaten floorboards. She couldn't sleep because of the box. If a box could have a spirit, then it was beginning to possess her. It seemed Randy had the same problem.

When he crept into her room an hour before dawn, Karin was sitting up, holding the little box in her hand and staring at the button.

"I knew you'd be awake," said Randy.

She was glad he was there, because she couldn't go on sitting alone any longer. She just had to tell somebody. She had to talk about it.

"I can't stop thinking about it," she told him. "I put it back in the puzzle box, and then I put the puzzle box under my bed, but I could still see it there in my mind. It's like a photograph that won't go away. Then I put it in the hall, but that didn't help, so I snuck outside when everyone was asleep and put it in our car. But no matter where I put it, I still kept seeing it."

"So you went back out to get it?" asked Randy

Karin nodded. They both stared at the button. Its gold face now seemed silvery blue in the dim moonlight.

"I don't want it anymore," said Karin. "You can have it."

Randy shook his head. "You keep it."

They stared at the button in silence.

I'm not going to push it, thought Karin, although every fiber of her body told her that she was going to do just that. It was like trying not to look at her grandfather's body when they opened the coffin in the chapel. No matter how hard she tried not to, she just had to look.

Randy seemed to read what she was thinking.

"Let me do it," he said.

"No." Karin pulled the box a few inches away from him. "I mean, it's just a superstition, right?" said Karin.

"Right."

"And if we push it, nothing will happen, and we can stop worrying about it and get back to sleep, right?"

"Right."

Karin slipped her finger across the smooth, cold surface. She rested it on the button.

She could hear her heart pounding, and swore she could hear Randy's as well. Silently, she cursed her grandfather for giving her the button.

"Get it over with," hissed Randy.

Karin took a deep breath, felt the cold metal beneath her finger tip . . . and pressed.

She held the button down, gritting her teeth, closing her eyes.

But nothing happened.

No explosions, no demons, nothing. Only the silence of the night, and faint snores coming from the other rooms.

Feeling stupid, they both breathed a deep sigh of relief. This was what Grandfather wanted, Karin was sure now. He wanted to show them how weak they truly were. He had called them stupid—was this his way of proving it? Was he that wicked?

Karin stared at the button a moment longer, her finger still firmly pressing it down. Finally, she relaxed and took her finger off of it.

"Well," she said as the button snapped back up, "I guess that's it. I guess nothing's going to hap—"

FLUSHIE

DUNCAN HELD HIS BREATH.

He always held his breath, and he had gotten quite good at it. But not good enough.

"I coulda had a C!" growled Brett Duggan when the assault began. "I needed a C on this test—I told you that!"

Duncan had squirmed and fought against Brett and Nate's powerful grip, but then Charlie had joined in. Duncan had no chance of fighting off three of them.

"Hold him!" yelled Nate, his voice echoing in the tiled bathroom.

It hadn't taken the three of them long to push Duncan to his knees.

"All you had to do, Duncan, was get a B," said Brett, pretending to be calm. "You know what a B is, don't you? Anything less than *90 percent!* But does Duncan Goldwater get a B? No. You get *104!* Like, how does someone get 104?"

"Extra credit!" Duncan screamed defiantly. He knew the answers to all the questions on that boneheaded math test, and no one was going to force him to lower his grade on purpose. It wasn't his fault the teacher graded on a curve like they sometimes did in high school. True, if Duncan weren't in the class the curve would have made Brett's miserable 67 a C-minus instead of a D. But it wasn't Duncan's job to make sure morons like Brett Duggan, Nate Carver, and Charlie Mintz passed math, or science, or English.

With Duncan's head hovering over the toilet, he was completely at their mercy, and the ritual began—a ritual that was passed on from grade to grade—a ritual that kept the bullies in charge—and Brett, Nate, and Charlie were really good at being bullies. Duncan suspected it was the only thing they *were* good at.

It happened like it always happened. And Duncan held his breath.

Brett gave Nate a thumbs-up and yelled, "Flush!"

Nate lifted his foot and stomped down on the shiny metal lever.

Grrissshh! Water gushed in Duncan's face like a great flood—not from a tank, but straight from the water pipes built into the walls of the old school bathroom. The newer rest room in the science wing had more water-efficient toilets, but when you needed to deliver someone a really good flush, the first-floor boys room was the best place to do it.

"Flush!" ordered Brett.

Grrissshh!

The water swirled around Duncan's head—colder this time, coming from deeper in the pipes. Duncan could no longer hold his breath. He opened his mouth to take a gasp of air, but mostly he got a mouthful of chlorinated water. It was the same lousy-tasting water that bubbled out of the faucets and water fountains around school, but telling himself that didn't make Duncan feel any better.

"Flush!" commanded Brett. Nate stomped on the lever a third time.

Grrissshh!

The water exploded in his face again, and at last the three flushmasters were satisfied. The water found its level in the bowl, and Brett lifted Duncan's head from the toilet by his sopping wet hair. Humiliated, Duncan stumbled to a dusty corner of the bathroom and slid to the floor like a rag doll.

At fourteen, Duncan still felt like crying whenever they flushed him, but he held the tears back. Crying was what they wanted. From the time he was six his classmates wanted to see him break. He could not give in.

"I'm really tired of you, Flushie," said Brett, kicking the toilet seat down for emphasis. The mighty porcelain bang was still echoing when he stormed out. Charlie followed him, laughing, but Nate lingered at the door.

"Duncan," he said, "you're such a waste of life." And then he was gone, letting the door squeak closed behind him.

Duncan knew how he must have looked, crumpled there in the corner of the bathroom, wet from his shirtpocket up. Pathetic.

But I'm not pathetic! his inner voice screamed. *They make me look this way! They make me feel this way!*

What was the use? Duncan cradled his head in his hands. He wasn't the only A student in school; there were lots of others. Maybe the walking brain-dead like Brett grumbled about the smarter kids behind their backs, but those other smart kids were respected. They were well liked by everyone, and none of them—*none* of them—ever got the flush.

That honor was reserved for one boy alone: Duncan Goldwater.

Why me? Duncan would always wonder . . . but he was smart enough to know why.

It was because he was Flushie. He had always been Flushie. If he were a D student, he would *still* be Flushie. There would always be a reason to give him the old swirling shampoo, because from the first day that he let them over-power him that's who he became. There were kids in school who didn't even know him by any other name. Just Flushie.

The door creaked open. And the humiliation contin-ued, only now it had a different face.

It was Sandra Martell.

He didn't want her to see him this way. He didn't want anyone to see him this way, especially not her.

She stepped in slowly and gingerly, as if the white floor tiles were eggshells—as if the floor of the boys room was filled with invisible mines that only a girl could set off.

Duncan stood up immediately. His shoes slipped on the wet floor, but he recovered quickly, grasping onto an old radiator coil.

Sandra stood a few feet away, not saying anything yet, so Duncan said something. Something stupid.

"This is the boys room," he offered, and deep in his mind the little guy who ran things bashed his moronic A-plus brain with a hammer for being so dumb.

"I know," said Sandra. "Are you okay?"

"Yeah," said Duncan. "No problem."

Sandra still kept her distance. Duncan tried to remember if she had ever been one of the flushers before. Had she ever been there watching and laughing like so many others did—others who Duncan thought were friends? Well, maybe she had been one of them before, but she wasn't laughing now, and that was something.

"Brett, Nate, and Charlie . . . they can be such creeps," she said.

"Brett, Nate, and Charlie," echoed Duncan, "have the combined IQ of a soccer ball."

Sandra laughed. "A *retarded* soccer ball." She shrugged. "Still, they're not all bad. They're just jealous. I mean, remember at the science fair, how they smashed the electronics on your seeing-eye bicycle, because all they had were dumb things like baking soda volcanoes? See—they're mad 'cause they can't be as smart as you."

Duncan shrugged, then mumbled, "Maybe."

"And anyway," said Sandra, "someday you'll be designing supercomputers or something, and making lots of money. They'll be lucky just to work for you, right?"

"I guess," said Duncan.

"So you see, Flushie, it's not so bad."

"Duncan!" he said a little too loudly. "My name is Duncan."

Sandra backed away a bit, grimacing at her mistake. "Sorry, Duncan. It's just . . . I don't know . . . we've all gotten used to the name. It's just a nickname. It doesn't mean anything. I'll call you Duncan from now on."

She said his name as if it were a foreign word, heavy and hard to push out.

For lack of a better idea, Duncan held out his hand for her to shake. "Thanks, Sandra," he said. "Thanks for coming in and talking to me."

She looked at his outstretched hand with silent

dread. His hands were still wet from being flushed, so Duncan dried them on his pants, then held out his hand again. Sandra *still* wouldn't shake it.

She took an uncomfortable step back. "I've never been in a boys room before," she said. "I'd better go."

She left much more quickly than she had come in, and Duncan dropped his arm.

Did she really care what happened to him, or was it just pity? Was he really that untouchable to a girl like Sandra? He had seen her dissect a frog in science class, and on a field trip he'd seen her dig for clams in briny muck up to her elbows. But his hands she would not touch.

Outside, the sound of feet heading to fourth period gave way to the second bell, and then silence.

In that silence Duncan thought about how he would get them back. He would get them *all* back. There was no doubt of that. The very thought made him feel much, much better.

Duncan got up and stood before the warped bathroom mirror. He pulled a comb from his pocket and combed his hair, determined to step out of the bathroom with some dignity.

Cheshire Tower stood majestically at the corner of Second Avenue and Eighty-fourth Street. Anywhere else on the planet its twenty-seven floors would have been impressive, but this was New York, so it was dwarfed by taller skyscrapers on three of its four sides.

Duncan's apartment had never had a chance at a decent view, being on the second floor. "Your mother's afraid of heights"—that was his father's excuse for putting their home nose-level with the diesel exhaust pipes that rumbled by on the street below all day long. "You want a view?" his father would say. "Then go up to the pool on the roof." But Duncan had better things to do today.

His pockets stuffed with allowance money he had been saving for weeks, Duncan left the building and turned up Eighty-fourth Street, where the beige bricks of Cheshire Tower gave way to the dark bricks of the old five-story low-rises that filled the rest of the street. Now that summer was just a week away, the pavement was teeming with activity. Duncan didn't know any of these people; they were just faces he passed on his way to his school every day. But he knew about Eugene. Everybody knew about Eugene.

Eugene was only twelve but was almost ready to shave. He was nearly two years younger than Duncan, but his voice was already changing. Eugene was simply never born to be a kid.

As always, Eugene was out on his stoop as if he were waiting for something. He usually was.

"Do I know you?" he asked in a thick New York accent when he saw Duncan approach.

"You're Eugene, right? You sell stuff, don't you?"

"I don't sell stuff," said Eugene, looking around cautiously. "I sell *items*. You need an item?"

"I hear you got great fireworks—I need some for Fourth of July."

"Well, why didn't you say so?"

A minute later they were down in a basement, where Eugene revealed a regular arsenal of fireworks. He walked around, pointing things out to Duncan. "You got your

Roman candles, you got your M-80s, you got your block-busters—and none of those namby-pamby legal ones—this is the old-fashioned stuff. These Roman candles here will blow a hole in your face the size of a baseball. Pretty cool, huh?"

"What about the blockbusters?"

"You kiddin' me?" He pointed to a collection of colorful cylinders, an inch in diameter and about two inches long. "Quarter stick of dynamite in each one—make a blast you can hear all the way to Jersey. Guaranteed to make a big splash with your friends."

"How much for the whole box?"

Eugene raised an eyebrow. "How much you got?"

"I can't believe it," said Brett. "I must be dead or something. Flushie actually got a C on the math final!"

Duncan overheard the conversation. Mr. Carbuckle, the math teacher, wanted to talk with him about the test, but Duncan didn't care. Carbuckle tossed out the lowest grade anyway, and this was definitely Duncan's lowest grade.

"You did it on purpose, didn't you?" asked Sandra, but Duncan just shrugged. "Maybe I just didn't study." He headed out into the hall, following Brett and his entourage of friends.

Brett spotted him and put his head into a headlock—Brett's idea of a friendly gesture. "Jeez, Flushie, you didn't have to do *that* bad on my account."

"Least I could do for you, Brett," said Duncan. "After all, you haven't flushed me for a whole month."

As everyone laughed, Duncan reached into his back-pack and pulled out a bundle of envelopes. "Listen, everybody. Since we'll all be going to different high schools next year, I wanted to have a party for Fourth of July. You can see the Central Park fireworks from the roof of my building."

Duncan reached into his backpack and handed Brett the first invitation.

The sports club on the top of Cheshire Tower had a fifty-foot indoor swimming pool—not all that big, but big enough for the twenty-seventh floor of an apartment building. There were windows all around it, but most impressive was the big window at the deep end, just six inches above the waterline. There was no deck at the deep end, and anyone who could bob his head high enough would get a glorious view of the city from the pool.

It had cost Duncan's father a small fortune to rent out the entire pool for the Fourth of July. Duncan promised to work all summer to pay it off, and by the time school ended, he had already lined up some odd jobs tutoring math and walking an old lady's five poodles. The work helped to pass the time from the end of school to the Fourth of July—two weeks that, to Duncan, seemed to stretch on forever.

Then, on that long-awaited Saturday evening, his schoolmates began to arrive in droves. Duncan couldn't believe that they all came!

"I never knew you had so many friends," remarked his mother.

"Yeah. It's amazing what pizza can do," said Duncan. And pizza there was. Everywhere. There was even one floating on a platter in the pool, looking like a jellyfish with pepperoni on it.

"This is great, Duncan," said Trevor—another flusher who had never said anything nice to him before. A girl named Melissa, who was famous for spreading vicious rumors about Duncan behind his back, scarfed down pizza and told him that he was the best.

But there was one guest who was not having a good time. Sandra sat in her green party dress, alone on the edge of a chaise lounge.

"You didn't tell me it was a pool party!" she said.

"Sorry, I forgot," Duncan lied. "If it makes you feel any better, I won't go swimming either."

Sandra smiled politely at his offer.

"You could help me ref the volleyball game," he suggested. Then he looked at his watch. It was already twenty minutes before nine, just the right time for the game. It would definitely be the best game ever.

When it got dark, Independence Day exploded in the skies over Cheshire Tower like a revolution. Duncan helped his dad set up the volleyball net across the width of the pool, and everyone except Duncan and Sandra played.

Brett, who was self-proclaimed captain of the deep-water team, hogged the ball and held several people under water until they came up coughing. This strategy seemed to work, because they creamed them. It was 8:56.

Duncan began to get just a bit edgy. "Rematch!" he called, but there were complaints that the sides weren't fair, and people began hopping out of the pool. To Duncan, that was completely unacceptable.

It was then that he slipped on the wet tiles of the

deck. He didn't fall in the pool, but the sight of old Flushie slipping was enough to plant a seed in everyone's mind. It only took one suggestion from Brett for that seed to take root.

"Taking up diving, Flushie?" razzed Brett. Everyone laughed, and Brett heaved himself out of the pool, heading around the deck toward Duncan. The others looked at one another and began smiling.

"Sure, I'll bet you could be an Olympic diver," said Charlie, jumping out of the pool.

And then Nate said what they were all thinking: "Let's throw Duncan in the pool!" There was outrageous commotion in the water as everyone climbed out and headed toward him. Panicked, Duncan looked for his parents, but they were probably out on the sun deck watching the fireworks.

Sandra saw what was happening and tried to stop it. But there were simply too many of them. Then she slipped, too, falling hard on her knees.

"*Flush-ie, Flush-ie, Flush-ie!*" they chanted as they approached. The useless lifeguard pointed and blew his whistle, but nobody listened. *Not now!* thought Duncan, looking at his watch. It was exactly one minute until nine!

Naturally, Brett was the first one to reach him, and the look on his face reminded Duncan why he had thrown this "party" to begin with. Brett looked like a lion about to devour an antelope. It was how he looked whenever he flushed Duncan.

Brett grabbed Duncan hard. Duncan resisted, but then he felt hands all over him lifting him off the ground, moving him closer to the water.

"*Flush-ie, Flush-ie, Flush-ie!*"

"No!" yelled Sandra, but she got tangled up in the mob as she tried to get them off Duncan.

"Flush-ie, Flush-ie, Flush-ie!"

They all heaved at once, and the force created enough momentum to take them all in, like a single beast with a dozen arms and legs.

Far away a church bell began to chime nine o'clock, and an odd sound echoed under the surface of the Cheshire Tower pool, like a submarine struck by a torpedo. The big window just above the deep end rattled violently.

By the time everyone came up for air, it was clear something strange was going on. The water was moving all by itself.

While the others floundered, wondering what was going on, Duncan swam with all his might to the nearest ladder, held on with all his strength, and watched.

It didn't happen the way he had imagined it. He had thought there would be a whirlpool spinning around and around, but there wasn't. Instead, there was a wave in the deep end that rolled like the ocean surf but never got any closer. The water in front of that wave was dragged beneath the churning water like a powerful undertow.

"Wow, a wave pool!" shouted Charlie.

Nate, who was right underneath the big window at the deep end, was the first to find out exactly what was going on. First his head bobbed on top of the great rolling wave, then he was pulled beneath it. Without even having a chance to scream, he was pulled deep down in the pool, and before he knew what was happening, he was out in the cold night air, falling toward the taxi cabs twenty-seven floors below.

Everyone caught on quickly when Charlie disappeared, too. Then the screaming began. They all tried to fight the riptide pulling them to the deep end, but it was hopeless. One by one their screams were silenced, and they were pulled under as if into the mouth of a shark, then ejected from the building through a huge, jagged hole in the side of the pool.

Duncan watched with a sense of power he hadn't felt since the week before, when he had finished building the time bomb—the very bomb that had now blown a hole in both the pool and the outer wall of the building. It had been easier to build than any of his science projects. *I'll bet they heard that in Jersey, huh, Eugene?* he thought when the blast first went off.

The lifeguard and adults, who had rushed back to the pool, could do nothing but gawk and shriek as they watched kid after kid go under.

Melissa went, dragging the volleyball net with her, followed by several others. It was then that Sandra came floating by, her green party dress rippling around her like a lily pad. Duncan could not let *her* go. He had never intended for her to be in the water at all. He reached out his hand and she grabbed it—this time with no reservations. That in itself was something! He pulled her toward him and helped her hook her arms around the chrome pole of the pool ladder.

Now do you see? he thought. *Now do you see why I didn't want you to swim? You're the only one worth saving, Sandra. The only one!*

There was a roaring blast like the sound of a whale's blowhole, and they both turned to see that the water level had dropped far enough to reveal the top lip of the gaping hole. The rolling wave was gone, and all that remained was the water pouring down a bottomless water slide that spilled into the sky above Eighty-fourth Street.

Brett bobbed past Duncan, holding out his grubby hand. He locked eyes with Duncan. This time, Brett's eyes were the eyes of the antelope. "Help me," he pleaded.

Duncan held out his hand toward Brett, but instead of taking Brett's hand, Duncan closed his fingers into a fist and gave Brett a thumbs-up.

"Flush!" sneered Duncan. With that, the current caught Brett and pulled him to the hole, where he was permanently expelled.

Duncan looked to Sandra, who was screaming and shivering as she clung to the ladder.

"It's okay," he said.

He wanted to stop her from crying. He wanted to kiss her. Would she let him do that, knowing now how strong he really was? Strong enough to beat his enemies—strong enough to win once and for all. Duncan took one hand from the ladder and moved it toward her trembling cheek.

That's all it took.

His foot slipped from the rung, his hand slipped from the bar, and he was suddenly moving farther and farther away from Sandra. "Duncan!" she screamed. He tried to swim back to her, but it was too late. The current had him, and he felt himself being pulled toward the final flush of his life.

Trevor was still in the pool, fighting a battle with the foaming white water—a battle he lost. Trevor went down, then at last the hole locked its sights onto Duncan, pulling him toward it like a tractor beam. Helpless, he stopped fighting its powerful gravity and accelerated toward the black hole. Then, as if in slow motion, it ejected him out onto . . . city lights! All around, dazzling him! Wind, filling his ears, eyes, and mouth!

Far below, the traffic had already come to a screeching halt. Honking horns, screaming bystanders, and bursts from the Central Park fireworks filled the night. Duncan took in the amazing view as he fell, and he let out a final cry of victory, for he knew that all the others had gone before him. At least that was something!

As the ground raced up to meet him, Duncan threw out his arms and legs, riding the wind like a skydiver.

And he held his breath.

SCREAMING AT THE WALL

"OF COURSE I LOVE YOU," SAYS GRANDMA. "I LOVE YOU very, very much, Leslie."

Grandma stands inches away from the hallway wall. There is not so much as a picture on the wall, just white paint.

I can see her from my room. The way she stands there talking to the wall—it scares me.

"Let me give you a hug," says Grandma. She holds out her arm and grasps the air in front of her, as if she is hugging someone. But no one is there.

She's been talking to that wall for about a month now. It's not just the wall, though. She'll laugh at some joke that no one except her hears. She'll get angry at someone who's not even in the room. And she treats all of us as if we're invisible.

Dad hardly seems to notice anymore. He's too busy remodeling the house, even late at night. Each night I go to sleep to the sound of saws and hammers and drills.

Mom sits on the edge of my bed, and we talk about things. Lately, we just talk about Grandma.

"Sometimes it happens like that when you get old. People just sort of wind down," Mom tells me. "It's a part of life."

I think about that: *winding down*, like old gears . . . like our grandfather clock in the hall, which can never keep the right time. But Grandma's not a machine; she's a human being.

I think back to the times when Grandma was okay, before her mind started to slip. She was wonderful and warm and loving. She would take me to the movies and we would talk like the best of friends. But that was a long time ago. Now she's very different. My friends laugh at her, but there's nothing funny about it.

I hear a hammer banging away in the garage. In the kitchen, Grandma sits in the dark. I can hear her talking about the ice cream she's pretending to eat, and then she sings "Happy Birthday" to the empty room. I remember that my birthday is coming up next month.

"That's all right, honey," she says to the dark, empty room. "I don't mind wearing a party hat."

"Who is she talking to?" I ask Mom. "What is she seeing?"

"I don't think we'll ever know," says Mom.

I know what my birthday wish will be. I'll wish that Grandma had her mind back.

It is midnight. I hear Grandma. I leave my room and go into the living room, where Grandma sits in the green velvet chair, watching TV by moonlight. But the TV isn't on.

"They call this music?" she says. "A lot of noise if you

ask me. And look at them—grown men with pink hair."

She reaches down beside her and moves her hand back and forth. It takes me a moment to figure out what she's doing. She's petting a dog. But we don't have a dog.

"And what's the point of smashing the guitars?" she says, pointing at the dark TV. "This isn't music; it's a circus."

"Grandma, can you hear me?" I ask.

She looks through me as if I'm not even there. Then, suddenly, she gasps in shock and jumps to her feet. She feels around for the walls as if she's blind.

"I'll go get candles," she says, and then shakes her head with a sigh.

"All this rain," she says. "I've never seen it rain like this." But outside the stars are out and the moon is bright. It isn't raining—not a drop.

Dad works hard every weekend, building our new rec room. He pretends that nothing is happening. Grandma is his mother; it must be hard for him to see her like this. I bet he wonders if it will happen to him.

Anyway, he doesn't like to talk about it, but I keep asking because I want answers. I miss the way Grandma used to be.

"It started about five years ago," Dad finally says, resting from his work and drinking a Coke. "I remember, I first noticed something was wrong when she started laughing at a joke before the punch line. She just walked away, not even hearing the rest of the joke. Then she would start waking up at all hours of the night. She would go and make herself breakfast and talk at the breakfast table as if we were all there." He shook his head. "It was two o'clock in the morning. Anyway, pretty soon she was living in a whole different world from us."

Dad wipes the sweat from his brow. "She needs us to take care of her now. Okay, Leslie?"

I nod quietly, sorry I made him talk about it.

Dad goes back to his work, burying himself in the room he's adding on, trying not to think about Grandma. I watch as he takes a heavy sledgehammer and swings it at the hall wall, over and over, creating a huge hole that will become the doorway to our new rec room.

One night before the rec room is finished, Grandma starts screaming at the wall again.

"How dare you!" she screams. "I'm your own flesh and blood!"

The others race in to find her standing in the unfinished rec room. "You're going to put me in a sanitarium?" she screams at the drywall in the corner. "That's what you're going to do? I'm not crazy!"

"I can't take this anymore, Carl!" my mom screams at my dad. She storms out of the room in tears.

Dad follows her, trying to calm her down, and I'm left alone with Grandma.

There's no electricity in the rec room yet. The only light comes from the hallway and from the bright, full moon. I watch Grandma staring out of the picture window, as if she can see something in the dark, as if she can see the river that the window overlooks. All I can see is darkness.

There are tears in her eyes. Even though she is standing right next to me, she seems so far away. So alone.

"Grandma," I ask. "Do you love me?"

"I wish it would stop raining," she says, looking up at the clear, starlit sky. "All this rain, it can't be good for the soil."

"Could you just give me a hug, Grandma—just one hug, like you used to?"

Then, for a moment, I get the feeling that we have had this conversation before. But the feeling is gone in an instant.

For my thirteenth birthday we have a small party with just a few friends. Dad tries to get us to wear stupid party hats, but no one wants to. Grandma sits alone on a folding chair out in the unfinished rec room, staring at the unpainted wall across the room, occasionally chuckling to herself.

We all eat ice cream and everyone sings "Happy Birthday"—everyone except Grandma. A few minutes later I notice that one of my dumb friends has put a party hat on her. I go into the rec room and take the hat off.

"Have you ever seen the river like this?" Grandma says to the dry, sunny day. "All swollen from the rain? It has to stop raining soon."

For a strange moment, as I hold that party hat in my hands, I get the feeling again that I've done this before . . . but I know I haven't.

Party hat, I think. *Wasn't Grandma talking about a party hat a few weeks ago?* But everyone calls me back into the living room to open my presents, so I don't think about it anymore.

For my birthday I get a puppy.

The next night it begins to rain. Troubled by the thunder and lightning, I stay up late and watch TV with Mom and Dad in the living room. Magoo, my new dog, sits by the side of the green velvet chair. On TV a rock band plays wild music. Mom and Dad think it's awful, but I kind of like it. And then I notice . . .

The guys in the band all have pink hair . . . and at the end of the song they smash their guitars.

A chill runs through my body. I look for Grandma, but she is not in the room.

"What's wrong, Leslie?" asks Mom. "Are you all right?"

"I don't know," I say. "I just feel . . . funny."

Bam! The thunder crashes at the same moment the lightning hits, and the house is plunged into darkness.

Dad is up immediately. "I'll get the candles," he says. He feels around for the walls in the dark, like a blind man.

A few minutes later, with a candle in my hand, I search the house for Grandma. I find her in the garage, looking through boxes of old photos.

"Can't leave these behind," she says. "Have to take them with me."

"Grandma," I ask, just beginning to understand. "Where are you? What do you see?"

"Barry, you and your family should never have come to visit with the weather like this," says Grandma. "You should have told them not to come, Carl. You can do what you like, but I'm not taking the chance. I'm getting my stuff, and I'm getting out. Before it's too late."

I can tell she's talking to my Dad and Uncle Barry— but Uncle Barry and his family live a thousand miles away in Michigan, and they haven't visited us for years. Yet Grandma's talking to them like they're in the room.

And suddenly I realize what's wrong with Grandma.

"Grandma," I say. "I know what's happening. I understand now."

"Leslie, your imagination is running away with you," says Dad. He's sitting in the rec room holding a candle. The lights have been out for an hour now. I stand at the entrance to the rec room. Mom and Dad sit in a corner. They're talking about putting Grandma into a home or a sanitarium.

"No!" I insist. "It's true. Grandma is living in the future. She's not crazy."

"Get some rest," says Mom. "You'll feel better in

the morning."

"No, I won't!" I shout. "Don't you get it?" I stand in the doorway of the rec room. "This doorway used to be a wall—this used to be the wall that Grandma would talk to—but she wasn't talking to the wall, she was talking to *us* inside the rec room. Only the rec room hadn't been built yet! And when she was pretending to eat ice cream in the middle of the night, she was seeing my birthday party a month later. And when she watches the TV when it's off, she's seeing TV shows that won't be on for a whole month. I even caught her petting the dog *before* we had the dog. And remember when she stood in the rec room screaming into the corner about your wanting to send her away? Well, she was screaming into the corner you're sitting in right now! She *saw* the conversation you're having right now, and it really upset her!"

I clench my fists, trying to get Mom and Dad to understand. "Don't you see? Grandma's body might be stuck in the present, but her mind is living a month in the future." I pointed to the grandfather clock down the hall. "It's like how that clock always runs too fast. At first it's just a couple of minutes off, but if we don't reset it, it could run hours—even days—ahead of where it's supposed to be! Grandma's like that clock, only she can't be fixed!"

Lightning flashes in the sky, and Mom stands up. "I think this storm is giving us all the creeps. I'll feel better when it's over tomorrow."

"No," I say. "According to Grandma the storm goes on for weeks and weeks."

That's when we hear Grandma screaming.

We run into the bedroom to find Grandma thrashing

around the room, bumping into things. She clutches the bedpost, holding on for dear life, as if something is trying to drag her away. Mom and Dad try to grab her but she doesn't see them; she just keeps on thrashing and clinging to the bedpost, like a flag twisting in the wind.

"Barry!" she screams. "Hold on! Carl! Don't let go!"

Dad grabs her and holds her, but she is stronger than any of us realize. There is sheer terror in her eyes, and I try to imagine what she sees. "Holly's gone, Carl—Holly, Barry, Alice, the twins, they're all gone—there's nothing you can do! Now you have to save yourself! No, don't let go! No!"

She screams one last bloodcurdling scream that ends with a gurgling, as if she were drowning. Then, silence.

And that's when I know Grandma is gone.

She's still breathing, her heart is still beating, but she is limp and her eyes are unseeing. Her mind has died, but her body doesn't know it yet. It will in several weeks, I think.

Suddenly, the only sound I hear is the falling rain and the rushing of the river a hundred yards beyond our backyard.

That was almost a month ago. Now I stand in my room, shoving everything I care about into my backpack, making sure I leave room for Magoo. I don't let Mom and Dad know what I'm doing. I can't let them know, or they would stop me.

In the rec room, which has been painted, carpeted, and furnished, Mom makes up the sofa bed. "Uncle Barry and Aunt Alice won't mind sleeping on this," says Mom, patting the bed. "The twins can sleep in your room," she tells me. "You can stay with us. It's only a week—I don't want to hear you complaining."

But I'm not complaining.

"Isn't it wonderful that they're coming all the way from Michigan to spend some time with us?" says Mom. "After all these years?"

"I just wish we had better weather. I've never seen it rain this much," says Dad, coming in the room. "It can't be good for the soil."

That night, I give Mom and Dad a powerful hug and kiss good night, holding them like I'll never let them go. Then, after everyone's asleep, I go into Grandma's room. She lies in bed, as she has for a whole month now. Not moving, barely even breathing.

I give her a hug also, and then I climb out of the window into the rain.

It is raining so hard that in moments I am drenched from head to toe. I am cold and uncomfortable, but I'll be all right.

Tonight I will run away. I don't know where I will go; all I know is that I have to leave. Even now, I can hear the river churning in its bed, roaring with a powerful current ready to spill over its banks.

Tomorrow, after Uncle Barry's family arrives, there will be a disaster. It will be all over the news. There will be special reports about how the river overflowed and flooded the whole valley. The reports will tell how dozens of homes were washed away, and how hundreds of people were killed.

I can't change any of that, because Grandma already saw it. She saw my mom, my dad, my uncle, my aunt, and my cousins taken away by the flood. Then, finally, the waters took her as well. She saw it more than a month ago.

But on that day when we watched her in her bedroom, holding on to her bedpost, torn by waters that we could not see, there was one name she didn't mention. She didn't mention me. And if I wasn't there, then at least one member of my family will have a future.

So tonight I take the high road out of town. And tomorrow I won't watch the news.

ALEXANDER'S SKULL

IT STARTED WITH MY MOM, MANY YEARS AGO.

My mom has a temper, you see, and one of the things that really got her up in a rage was the post office. If something took too long to arrive at our house, she would bawl out the mailman, as if it were his fault. If a card she sent missed somebody's birthday, she would go to the post office and demand her postage back.

The thing that irritated my mom most about the post office was misdelivered mail, and she had a good reason for that one: The Mortimer Museum.

It was just dumb luck that the guy who founded that strange little natural history museum had the same last name as we did. We weren't related, my dad always reminded me. Still, without fail, a few times a year we would end up with a package at our doorstep that was supposed to go to the museum.

For my mom, it was just another postal nuisance—until the birthday incident. Then it became a regular obsession with her.

I was about four or so. It was my mom's thirtieth birthday, and we had relatives and friends from all over the county show up to surprise her. Everything was going along just fine until she started opening the presents—first the ones from the people who were there, then the ones that had come in the mail.

Perhaps if she had looked at the address on the package, it might not have happened, but she didn't. So, right in front of more than forty guests, in the middle of a birthday party, my mother opened a box, reached in, and pulled out an armful of African centipedes.

The scream could be heard throughout the county. She shook her hand, shrieking, and flung the centipedes across the room, where they landed on slices of birthday cake and in people's hair. The angry centipedes began to bite, and panic erupted. Needless to say, the party was ruined. The centipedes had scattered so far across the room that we were still finding them in dark corners weeks later.

The centipedes, of course, were supposed to go to the Mortimer Museum for their exotic insect exhibit, and not to the Mortimer family. The post office, naturally, bent over backward and took full responsibility, offering to give my mother free postage for the rest of her life if she would just never mention it again. But it was too late.

From that day forward, we were at war with the museum and the post office. The poor mailman went to great pains to make sure we didn't get any of the museum's mail, but sometimes something slipped through. When it did, whatever it was—whatever it was—we kept it. Soon we had quite our own little museum in our basement: fragments of dinosaur bones, a meteorite, petrified wood.

But nothing we ever received was like the package we got one Halloween.

You have to understand, Halloween is a very special holiday for me. Most of the year I get teased for being sort of creepy and spending so much time alone, but on Halloween I can be myself and it's perfectly normal!

So that night I was in a rush to get out and stalk through the streets like a ghoul, striking terror into the heart of anyone foolish enough to answer their door, when a package arrived on our porch. I took it inside and quickly tore off the brown paper, pulled open the box, and like an idiot, reached inside to find out what it was.

My hand touched something cold, hard, and dirty. I quickly pulled my hand back and saw that it was covered with something black and sooty.

"Mom?" I called, feeling the shivers already climbing up past my elbow to my shoulder.

Mom came downstairs, took one look at the box, and heaved a big sigh. Then she peeled back the paper to reveal what at first looked like a dark rock. But when she reached in to pull it out, she came face to face with a human skull.

It was old—it must have been—because it was black and covered with ash. It was missing its jawbone.

"No way!" I said, not sure whether to be disgusted or excited. "It must be for the exhibit on Early Man."

Mom looked into its empty eyes bravely. "Splendid. Just what we need for Halloween. I'll go get a candle."

That night, the skull sat on our porch with a candle inside its empty head, like a human jack o'-lantern.

Like the other things in our basement, this was something we were going to keep—no matter how much the museum wanted it back. But the museum never came asking for it, and instead of ending up in the basement, it ended up in my room.

I can't say why I wanted the skull in my room. I was a little bit scared of it, but not as scared as I thought I would be. I liked the way it sat on my shelf and watched me. Also, since I didn't have many friends, it made me feel less alone.

My dad would look at

the skull and shake his head. "Alex," he would ask, "how did you get to be so strange?" That's what he said when I first got Octavia, my pet tarantula, and when I decided that I would wear only black to school.

"If you're going to keep that thing, Alex," he said, "you ought to clean it."

So I did. I carefully wiped off the ash and polished the cold, hard bone until it was a smooth granite gray. Then I put it back on my shelf next to Clovis, my Venus's-flytrap.

Late at night, when I couldn't fall asleep, I would

look at the skull. It seemed to be holding some kind of vigil in the dim moonlight, watching me as I watched it. *Who were you?* I would ask. *Were you a caveman? Were you killed by a mastodon during the hunt? Or are you the missing link?* The skull, to whom I wanted to give a name but somehow never could, never answered—it just sat there, watching silently.

Several weeks later it disappeared.

I spent an hour searching for it all around the house. Mom wasn't very helpful. "You're so disorganized," she said. "I always told you you'd lose your head if it weren't attached to your neck."

The skull wasn't in the basement, or in any of the bedrooms or closets. I knew there had to be a sensible explanation. Turns out the explanation was so sensible it was disappointing.

You see, my dad is a dentist, and his office is right across the street in a little minimall. When I went out to see if he knew what had happened, I saw my skull sitting there propped up on the dental chair, like a patient who had been X-rayed one too many times.

"Sorry. I should have told you," said Dad. "I borrowed him to recalibrate my X-ray machine. It's been giving me trouble." He showed me a dozen X-rays of the skull, all blurry and out of focus. He took one more shot with his big camera and handed me back my skull.

"This should do it," he said. "Thanks."

When he developed the X-ray a few minutes later, the teeth were in absolute clear focus, just like any other dental X-ray . . . so much like any other X-ray that Dad seemed a little bit disturbed. He went over to the skull and picked it up from the pillow it was resting on.

"You say he was prehistoric?" asked Dad.

"Yeah," I said. "I mean, he must be. Why else would he be going to the museum?"

Then Dad flipped the skull over and looked at the upper teeth, all of which were still there. He poked at them with a dental instrument. "Since when did prehistoric man have dental fillings?" he said, raising his eyebrows at me.

That afternoon I went down into the basement and found the box the skull had come in. Inside, I found the original wrapping. The faint brown lettering was not addressed to the museum, as we had thought. It was addressed to me— Alexander Mortimer.

There was a return address, but no name. The return address simply read "475 St. Cloud Lane, Billingsville."

It was a Saturday, so I decided to ride my bike over to Billingsville, only about ten miles away. I just had to see who had sent me this skull, and why.

Billingsville is a town with lots of old places and lots of new places. I got a map from the gas station, but try as I might, I couldn't find St. Cloud Lane.

"Ain't no St. Cloud Lane in Billingsville," an old timer told me. "Not that I can remember, and I can remember quite a lot."

Eventually I gave up and decided to head home

before it got dark. I rode through the winding streets of the new developments, wondering where on earth they were going to get all the people to fill these new homes.

That's when I saw it.

On a pole on a corner where two streets crossed were two signs—St. Andrew and St. Cloud Lane.

I sucked wind for a second, feeling kind of light-headed. Then I rode my bike down the lane. The entire street was filled with huge cement foundations, ready for construction crews. *The homes on St. Cloud Lane had not yet been built!*

It was dark by the time I got home, and the cold day had slipped into a frigid night.

"You missed dinner," said Mom, "Where were you?"

But I didn't answer her. I went right down into the basement and straight to the package the skull had come in. I looked for the postmark on the package. October twenty-eighth. But the year was smudged out, and there was no way of telling whether the package was mailed this year, last year . . . or some year that had not yet come.

That night, back in my room, I stared and stared at my "friend" sitting on the shelf. I went up to him and looked deep into those hollow eyes, eyes that seemed so strange, and yet so very familiar.

At three in the morning I slipped out of the house and crossed the street. Snow was falling and sticking to the dry ground. There would be several inches by morning. My feet left dark prints in the thin layer of white as I went to Dad's office. There, I unlocked the door with his keys and disabled the alarm.

The X-ray machine looked like a one-eyed beast in the corner of the examining room. I tried not to look at it. I went to my dad's office, and I looked around with my flashlight until I found the skull's X-rays still sitting on his desk. I took the most focused one and put it in my jacket pocket. Then I went to the files, found the folder I was looking for, and pulled it out. It was filled with dental records and X-rays.

I pulled out the skull's X-rays from my pocket and compared it to the X-rays in the folder.

They say you can identify human remains by dental records. It must be true, because the match was absolutely perfect.

I took a second look at the name on the file, and finally understood why it had been so hard for me to find a name for the skull. It was because the skull already had a name—it was the name that appeared on the file.

Alexander J. Mortimer.

As I reached up and felt my own cheekbones, and the shape of my eye sockets, and the ridges on my own front teeth, I finally realized why that head bone sitting on my shelf had, from the beginning, felt so very, very familiar.

In the morning Dad said we ought to take the skull to the police.

"They have ways of identifying these things," he said. "Who knows who it might be?"

But I told him that I had already gotten rid of it. "I gave it a proper burial out in the woods," I said, shrugging my shoulders.

He looked at me and shook his head. "How *did* you get to be such a strange kid?" he asked. Since my father was never the type of person to mess with matters involving human skulls, he believed me, and it was never brought up again.

Only I didn't bury it.

I don't know who sent me the skull. I don't know how, but it was sent, and I am charged with its keeping. Dad thinks I'm spending too much time alone lately, and that maybe if we moved I'd make some friends. He's heard that there are some nice homes going up in Billingsville—and he intends to buy one. I already know what our address will be.

And so at night, when everyone else is asleep, I take the skull out of its secret hiding place beneath the floorboards of my room and I put it back on my shelf. Then I lie awake, gazing at my silent soul mate resting on that shelf, and coldly wait for the day when I find myself on the other side of those dark, dark eyes, looking out.

SAME TIME NEXT YEAR

IN A VAST UNIVERSE, TOWARD THE EDGE OF A SPINNING galaxy, on a small blue planet flying around the sun, in a place called Northern California, lives a girl who is quite certain that the entire universe revolves around her. Or at least she acts that way. In fact, if an award were given out for acting superior, Marla Nixbok would win that award.

"I was born a hundred years too early," she often tells her friends. "I ought to be living in a future time where I wouldn't be surrounded by such dweebs."

To prove that she is ahead of her time, Marla always wears next year's fashions and hairstyles that seem just a bit too weird for today. In a college town known for being on the cutting edge of everything, Marla is quite simply the Queen of Fads at Palo Alto Junior High. Nothing and nobody is good enough for her, and for that reason alone, everyone wants to be her friend.

Except for the new kid, Buford, who couldn't care less.

Buford and Marla meet on the school bus. It's his first day. As fate would have it, the seat next to Marla is the only free seat on the bus.

The second he sits down, Marla's nose tilts up, and she begins her usual grading process of new kids.

"Your hair is way greasy," she says. "Your clothes look like something out of the fifties, and in general, you look like a Neanderthal."

Several girls behind them laugh.

"All else considered, I give you an F as a human being."

He just smiles, not caring about Marla's grade. "Hi, I'm Buford," he says, ignoring how the girls start laughing again. "But you can call me Ford. Ford Planct."

Ford, thinks Marla. She actually likes the name, against her best instincts. "Okay, F-plus—but just because you got rid of the 'Bu' and called yourself 'Ford.' "

"Didn't you move into the old Wilmington place?" asks a kid in front of them.

"Yeah," says Buford.

The kid snickers. "Sucker!"

"Why? What's wrong with the place?" asks Ford, innocently.

"Nothing," says Marla, "except for the fact that it used to belong to old Dr. Wilmington, the creepiest professor Stanford University ever had."

Ford leans in closer to listen.

"One day," says Marla, "about seven years ago, Wilmington went into the house . . . and never came out." Then she whispers, "No one ever found his body."

Ford nods, not showing a bit of fear.

"Personally," says Marla, trying to get a rise out of him, "I think he was killed by an ax murderer or something,

70

and he's buried in the basement."

But Ford only smiles. "I wouldn't be surprised," he says. "There's a whole lot of weird things down in our basement."

Marla perks up. "Oh yeah? What sort of things?"

"Experimental things, I guess. Gadgets and stuff. Does anyone know what sort of research this Professor Wilmington was doing when he disappeared?"

No one on the bus responds.

Ford smiles, and then stares straight at Marla. "By the way," he says, pointing to her purple-tinted hair and neon eye shadow, "you've got to be the weirdest-looking human being I've ever seen."

Marla softens just a bit. "Why, thank you, Ford!"

Marla peers out of her window that night. Through the dense oak trees she can see the old Wilmington house farther down the street. A light is on in an upstairs window. She wonders if it's Ford's room.

Like Marla, Ford is trapped out of his time, only *he* belongs in the past, and she belongs in the future. It's not as if she likes him or anything. How could she like him—he is a full geek-o-rama nausea-fest. But she can use him. She can use him to get a look at all those dark, mysterious machines in his basement.

Marla smiles at the thought. Using people is a way of life for her.

And so the very next afternoon, Marla fights a blustery wind to get to Ford's house. By the time she arrives, her punked-out hair looks even worse, for the wind has stood every strand on end. She likes it even better now.

"Thanks for coming over to help me study," says Ford as he lets her in. "I mean, moving in the middle of the school year sure makes it hard to catch up."

"Well, that's just the kind of person I am," says Marla. "Anything I can do to help a friend."

Marla looks around. The furniture is so tacky, it makes her want to gag. The living-room sofa is encased in a plastic slipcover. Ford's mother vacuums the carpet wearing a polka-dot dress, like in "I Love Lucy." For Marla, it's worse than being in a room filled with snakes.

"It's noisy here," says Ford. "Let's go study in my room."

Marla shudders. Who knows what terrors she'll find there?

"How about the basement?" she asks.

"It's creepy down there," says Ford.

"You're not scared, are you?"

"Who, me? Naw."

Marla gently takes his hand. "C'mon, Ford . . . we need a nice quiet place to study."

Ford, who has taken great pains not to be affected by the things Marla says or does, finally loses the battle. He takes one look at her hand holding his and begins to blush through his freckles. "Oh, all right."

While the rest of the house has been repainted and renovated, the basement has not changed since the day Wilmington disappeared. All of the old man's bizarre stuff is down there. Maybe Wilmington himself is down there somewhere, just a dried-out old skeleton lurking behind a heavy machine. What if they were to find him? How cool would that be?

As they descend the rickety stairs, Marla grips Ford's hand tightly, not even realizing she is doing so. Ford's blush deepens.

"Gosh, I thought you didn't even like me," says Ford.

Marla ignores him, blocking out the thought, and looks around. "What is all this stuff?"

"That's what I've been trying to figure out," says Ford.

Everything is shrouded in sheets and plastic tarps. Strange shapes bulge out. They look like ghosts, lit by the flickering fluorescent light. There is a warped wooden table in the middle of it all. Ford drops his school books down on the table and a cloud of dust rises. It smells like death down there—all damp and moldy. The walls are covered with peeling moss, and they ooze with moisture.

"We can study here," says Ford, patting the table. But Marla is already pulling the sheets off the machines.

Whoosh! A sheet flutters off with an explosion of dust, revealing a dark, metallic, multi-armed thing that looks like some ancient torture device.

"I wouldn't touch that," says Ford.

Marla crooks her finger, beckoning him closer. Her nails are painted neon pink and blue with tiny rhinestones in the center of each one. She leans over and whispers in Ford's ear, "If you really want to be my friend, you'll help me uncover all these machines."

Ford, his blush turning even deeper, begins to rip off the sheets.

When they're done, a cloud of dust hangs in the air like fog over a swamp, and the machines within that dusty swamp appear like hunched monsters ready to pounce. All they need is someone to plug them in.

Ford sits at the table and studies the old professor's notes and lab reports. But Marla is studying something else—the knobs and switches on the grotesque and fantastic devices are what grab her attention. They might not find Wilmington's body down there, but Marla is happy. This is already more interesting than anything she has done in quite a while.

She joins Ford at the scarred table, going through the professor's old notes page by page.

Hyperbolic Relativistic Projection.

Metalinear Amplitude Differentials.

It makes little sense to them, and Ford has to keep looking things up in a dictionary.

At last, with the help of the professor's notes, they're able to figure out what most of these machines are supposed to do.

The one with a metallic eyeball looking down from a tall stalk is a waterless shower that can dissolve dirt from your skin by sonic vibrations. But according to Wilmington's footnote, it doesn't work; it dissolves your skin, instead of the dirt.

The device with iron tentacles growing from a steel pyramid is supposed to turn molecular vibrations into electricity. It works, but unfortunately it also electrocutes anyone who happens to be standing within five feet of it.

Another device—a hydrogen-powered engine—was supposed to revolutionize the automotive industry. According to a letter the professor received from the chairman of one of the big car companies, the engine nearly blew up half the plant when they turned it on.

In fact, none of the things Wilmington made worked properly. Not the refractive laser chain saw, or the lead-gold phase converter, or even the self-referential learning microprocessor.

"No wonder no one from the university ever came by to collect all this stuff," Marla complains. "It's all junk."

Then Marla sees the doorknob. She hadn't noticed it before because it's in a strange place—only a foot or so from the ground, half hidden behind Wilmington's nonfunctioning nuclear refrigerator.

When Ford sees it, his jaw drops with a popping sound. "A tiny door! Do you think Wilmington shrunk himself?"

"Don't be a complete gel-brain," says Marla, brushing her wild hair from her face. "It's just a root cellar. But Wilmington might be in there . . . what's left of him, anyway."

The temptation is too great. Together they push the heavy refrigerator aside, grab the knob, and swing the door wide.

An earthy smell of dry rot wafts out, like the smell of a grave. The door is two feet high, and inside it is pitch black. Together, Marla and Ford step into the root cellar and vanish into darkness.

Through ancient spiderwebs they crawl until they find a dangling string. When they pull it, the room is lit by a single dim bulb that hangs from an earthen ceiling six feet from the ground.

There are no dead bodies down there. The smell is a sack of potatoes that have long since gone to their maker.

But what surrounds them is enough to make their hearts miss several beats.

Razor-sharp gears, knifelike spokes, and huge magnets are frozen in position. The entire room has been converted into one big contraption, and in the center of it is a high-backed chair, its plush upholstery replaced by silver foil.

It looks like the inside of a garbage disposal, thinks Marla.

In the corner sits a pile of dusty notes, and on a control panel is an engraved silver plate that reads:

TEMPUS SYNCRO-EPICYCLUS

"What is it?" wonders Marla. She looks to Ford, whom she has already pegged to be a whiz at this scientific stuff.

Ford swallows a gulp of rotten, stale air. "I think it's a time machine."

It takes a good half hour for them to find the nerve to actually touch the thing. Ford sits on the floor most of that time, reading Wilmington's notes.

"This guy has page after page of physics formulas," Ford tells Marla. "He must have thought he was Einstein or something."

"But does it work?" she asks.

Ford furrows his brow. "I have no idea."

"There's one way to find out," she says, grabbing Ford's sweaty hand.

Together they run upstairs and find the perfect guinea pig; Ford's baby sister's teddy bear, Buffy. They bring Buffy down and set him on the silver chair.

"I don't know," says Ford. "Maybe we ought to know

everything about this machine before we start throwing switches."

"You can't ride a bike unless you get on and pedal," says Marla, "and you can't travel through time unless you throw the switch!"

"But—"

Marla flicks the switch. The gears begin to grind, the electromagnets begin to spin and hum. They duck their heads to keep from being decapitated by the spinning spokes. Static electricity makes Ford's greased hair stand on end like Marla's. The dangling bulb dims.

There is a flash of light, and Buffy the bear is gone, leaving nothing behind but the stinging odor of ozone in the air. The machine grinds itself to a halt.

Ford and Marla are left gasping on the ground.

"In-totally-credible!" screeches Marla. "Now let's bring it back!"

"That's what I was trying to tell you," explains Ford, catching his breath. "According to Wilmington's journal, time travel only works one way. You can go forward in time, but you can never come back."

"That's ridiculous! That's not the way it happens in the movies."

"Maybe time travel doesn't work the way it does in movies," suggests Ford.

But to Marla it doesn't matter at all. The point is that however time travel works, it *does* work.

Ford looks to see where the dial is set.

"According to this," he says, "we sent the bear three days into the future. If the bear reappears in that chair three days from now, we'll really know if this thing works."

"I hate waiting," says Marla, as she impatiently picks her rhinestoned nails.

Two days later, Marla's parents read her the riot act. That is to say, they sit her down and demand she change her ways, or else.

"Your mother and I are sick and tired of you being so disrespectful," says her father.

"What's to respect?" she growls at them. "Is it my fault I was born into a family of cavepeople?"

That makes her parents boil.

"That's it," says her father. "From now on you're going to stop acting like the Queen of Mars, and you're going to start acting like a normal human being. From now on, young lady, no more neon blue lipstick. No more ultraviolet hair. No more radioactive eye shadow. No more automotive parts hanging from your earlobes. N-O-R-M-A-L. Normal! Do you understand me? Or else you get no allowance! Zero! Zilch!"

"You're so backwards!" screams Marla, and she runs to her room and beats up her pillows.

Alone with her thoughts, it doesn't take her long to decide exactly what to do. Without so much as a good-bye, she takes a final look at her room, then climbs out of the window and heads straight to Ford's house.

The sky is clear, filled with a million unblinking stars, and a furious wind howls through the trees. It's a perfect night for time travel.

"Marla," Ford says. "I've been reading Wilmington's notes, and there's something not quite right."

"Don't be an idiot!" Marla shouts in Ford's face. "The machine works—we saw it! We're going and that's final."

"*I'm* not going anywhere," says Ford. "I'm not into future stuff, okay?"

"It figures," huffs Marla. "I'll go by myself, then."

She pulls open the basement door and stomps down the stairs. Ford follows, trying to talk some sense into her.

"There's lots of stuff I'm still trying to figure out," he says.

"Oh yeah?" She whirls and stares impatiently at him. "Like what?"

"Like the name of the machine," Ford says. "It bugs me. *Tempus Syncro-Epicyclus*. I looked up the word *Epicyclus* in the dictionary. It has something to do with Ptolemy."

"Tommy who?" asks Marla.

"Not Tommy, *Ptolemy*. He was an ancient astronomer who believed the Earth was the center of the universe, and the sun revolved around it!"

"So?" she hisses.

"So, he was wrong!" shouts Ford.

Marla shrugs. "What does that have to do with a twentieth-century genius like Wilmington? At this very moment, *he's* probably in the future partying away, and I plan to join him."

Marla impatiently crosses the basement toward the root-cellar door.

"Marla, the last person to touch that machine must have been Wilmington—and it was set for three days! If he went three days into the future, *why didn't he come back?*"

"What are you
getting at?"

"I don't know!" says
Ford. "I haven't figured it out
yet, but I will! Listen, at least
wait until tomorrow. If the bear
comes back on schedule, you can do
whatever you want."

"I can't wait that long. I've got

places to go!" shouts Marla.

"You're crazy!" Ford shouts back. "You're the type of person who would dive headfirst into an empty pool, just to find out how empty it is!"

Marla pulls open the root-cellar door, but Ford kicks it closed. The house rattles and moss falls from the peeling walls.

"This is my house, and that means it's my machine," he says. "I won't let you use it, so go home. Now!"

Marla turns her Day-Glo painted eyes to Ford and grits her teeth. "Why you slimy little sluggardly worm-brain! How dare you tell me what I can and cannot do! You think I care what you say, you 'Leave-It-to-Beaver' dweebistic troll? Marla Nixbok does what she wants, *when* she wants to do it, and if you won't throw the switch on that machine, I'll throw it myself!"

Still, Ford refuses to budge, so Marla takes her nails and heartlessly scratches his face, a maneuver she often uses when words no longer work.

Ford grabs his face and yelps in pain. Then he takes his foot away from the door.

"Fine," says Ford. "Go see the future. I hope you materialize right in the middle of a nuclear war!" With that, he storms to the stairs.

Good riddance, thinks Marla. Maybe she ought to travel fifty years into the future, just so she can find Ford as a shriveled old man and laugh in his wrinkled face.

Marla bends down and crawls into the root cellar.

At the top of the basement stairs, the truth finally strikes Buford Planct with such fury that it nearly knocks him down the stairs. If Marla uses that machine, her future won't be nuclear war. It'll be far, far from it.

"No!" he screams, and races back down the stairs.

In the root cellar, Marla turns the knob to "One Year." One year is a good first trip. After that, who knows? Decades! Maybe centuries! At last she'll be free to travel to whatever time and place she feels she belongs. The Queen of Time. She likes the sound of that.

Ford crawls into the root cellar, out of breath.

"Marla, don't!" he screams.

"Get lost!" she shrieks back.

"But I figured it out!"

"Good. Does the machine work?"

"Yes, it does, but—"

"That's all I need to know!" Marla flips the switch

and leaps into the silver chair. "See you next year!" she calls.

"Nooooooo!"

But Marla never gets to see the horror in Ford's eyes. Instead she sees a flash of light and is struck by a shock of pain as she is propelled exactly one year into the future, in this, the most exciting moment of her life.

In an instant she understands it all—and it is much worse than diving into an empty pool. Now she knows what Ford had been trying so desperately to tell her, because she is now very, very cold.

And she is floating.

Ford was right: the machine works all too well. She has traveled one year forward in time.

But she isn't the center of the universe.

And neither is the Earth.

Suddenly she remembers that the Earth revolves around the sun, and the sun revolves around the center of the galaxy, and the galaxies are flying apart at millions of miles per hour. Everything in the universe has been moving, except for Marla Nixbok. Marla has appeared in the *exact* location in space that she had been one year ago . . .

But the Earth has long since moved on.

Even the sun is gone—just one among many distant stars.

Now she knows exactly why Wilmington and Buffy the bear can never come back. And as her last breath is sucked out of her lungs by the void of space, Marla Nixbok finally gets what she has always wanted: a crystal-clear vision of her own future. Now, and forever.

NOT IT

IT BEGAN WAY BACK IN THIRD GRADE AND CONTINUED FOR four unbearable years. It was a game. A simple game. It should have been fun, and for most of the kids playing, it was. But not for Taylor Sloat—all because he didn't say two tiny little words fast enough. He'd never forget that terrible day. It was the first week of third grade, years and years ago. Everyone was out in the Thornhaven school yard.

"Let's play freeze tag," someone suggested.

"Not it! Not it! Not it!" everyone shouted.

Taylor had opened his mouth to yell "not it" just like all the others, but by the time the words made it to his lips, he was the only one left. And so Taylor was *it*, and he had been *it* ever since.

" 'It' runs in Taylor's family—just look at his father," Taylor's classmate Mickey Van Horn once said. Taylor knew exactly what Mickey meant, and it made him furious. His dad had certainly been through enough without being called "it" by pimply faced Mickey Van Horn, whose dad was a hotshot senator.

At Thornhaven School, if your father wasn't a senator he was a billionaire, and competition was a way of life. It was no different with freeze tag. Some schools might consider seventh grade too old for freeze tag, but not Thornhaven. Here, the game was a time-honored tradition, and fall was freeze tag season. When winter rolled around and snow covered the yard, the season officially ended. On that last day, Mickey Van Horn always wrote up the stats. He listed who was frozen, where they were standing, and, of course, who was *it*. Then, that page of stats would mysteriously disappear, only to resurface the following fall, when the game was continued from where it left off.

Taylor watched on that first day of seventh grade as Mickey Van Horn brought out the crumpled piece of paper that told everyone where they ought to be standing for this year's game.

"Who's it?" asked Rex McMillan, even though he knew the answer.

"I'm not sure," said Mickey, holding back his laughter. "Taylor? Do you have any idea who *it* could be?"

"No idea," said Taylor.

"Don't you remember?" said Mickey. "You're *always* it." Everyone else began to snicker.

"Hey, maybe he'll finally win this year," said Cody Werner, a kid whose greasy hair got greasier every year.

"Fat chance," said Eddie Tupperman, who knew a lot about fat, considering all the pizza he ate.

"So, are you ready to play, Taylor?" Mickey asked, flashing an ugly, yellow-toothed smile.

Taylor didn't answer, but Mickey knew the answer anyway. The game would go on.

The game was played in a corner of the oversized school yard. It was a blacktop yard, perfectly square and surrounded on all sides by a rusty fence that seemed half a mile high. The yard was huge—so big that even when it was filled with kids from kindergarten through twelfth grade, it still felt almost empty. Voices and sounds in the yard always seemed faint and far away, as if those noises were merely the ghosts of kids running, skipping, and playing.

The far northwestern corner was where the freeze tag game had always been, and today when Taylor began to cross the great expanse of the asphalt yard, he could already see the others waiting for him.

I hate them, thought Taylor as he crossed through the clusters of young girls playing jump rope. *I wish this game had never been invented.*

"Well, *it's* arrived," said Mickey.

Everyone who wasn't frozen from last year immediately ran to the fence, which was "base"—the only place where *it* couldn't get you.

"No fair!" shouted Taylor, looking at the stat sheet. "Most of you guys were frozen last year!"

But nobody volunteered to leave the fence.

"I know *you* were frozen, Eddie," said Taylor, pointing at Fat Eddie, who just shook his beefy head and said, "Was not."

"Just shut up, *it*," shouted Mickey Van Horn. "Let's start the game. Lunch hour is half over already." And with that, Mickey took three steps away from the fence, toward Taylor.

"C'mon, Taylor," taunted Mickey, "tag me—I dare you! Make me the first person this year to be frozen."

Mickey took one step closer, and Taylor couldn't

resist. He lunged at Mickey furiously, but Mickey dodged to the right. Taylor came down hard on his elbows, scraping them across the rough asphalt.

The game had begun, and kids began leaping from the fence out into the yard, the "battle zone." They would leer at Taylor, coming within inches of him, and Taylor would spin his arms, trying to tag at least one. But there were too many of them, and they were too fast. Finally, Fat Eddie got frozen—he was always the easiest to freeze—and then Taylor tagged a few more. But since only Taylor's hands could freeze and anyone else's hands could defrost, everyone was quickly set free.

The rules, Taylor had decided a long time ago, were unfair. How could one person be expected to freeze twenty kids, while those twenty kids *all* had the power to defrost one another?

Taylor had also realized long ago that the game wasn't meant to be fair.

Mickey Van Horn weaved around other kids, bounding, hopping, and laughing like a demonic elf. He would run up, wag his hand in Taylor's face, and slip just out of his reach before Taylor could tag him. Then Mickey would run around defrosting kids like crazy. On it went, and Taylor just grew redder in the face, and more and more exhausted.

Then, suddenly, Mickey stood just a few feet away. He wasn't bouncing, he wasn't running around—he was just standing there with a wide, grotesque smile that taunted: *Come and get me . . . I dare you.*

If there was anything in the world Taylor wanted to do at that moment, it was to tag Mickey so hard that he would go flying across the whole yard. With that and only that in his mind, he lunged at Mickey with all the might he had left.

And the bell rang.

He had tagged him! With tears of joy, Taylor fell to the ground triumphantly, basking in glory in spite of his skinned elbows.

That's when Mickey said, "Doesn't count."

"What?" Taylor was dumbstruck. "I got you right on the shoulder. Everyone saw it!"

"Doesn't count," said Mickey flatly. "You got me after the bell rang."

Everyone who was on the fence began to hurry off toward school. The frozen kids all thawed out and jogged off to class.

"*IT HAS TO COUNT!*" screamed Taylor. "It's like basketball! I was already in the air when the bell rang."

Mickey looked around at his buddies. "Say, guys, if Taylor tags me after the bell rings, does it count—even if he was in the air?"

Fat Eddie, Greasy Cody, and all the others shook their heads. "Naah, doesn't count."

"Sorry, Taylor," said Mickey. "Majority rules." He patted Taylor on the shoulder, as if he were Taylor's friend, and jogged off toward the school with the others.

The yard was emptying quickly now as kids funneled through the heavy steel doors into the ivy-covered school. Taylor was the last one left outside. He stood alone, playing the game over and over in his mind.

Behind him the fence rattled in the wind, and Taylor looked up to see fat tree branches that had grown in and around the links of the fence. The funny thing about those branches was that the trees they belonged to had been cut down years ago. Now the branches were permanently part of the fence, and could not be removed. The twisted pieces of dead wood were condemned to remain a part of the school yard forever. Taylor wondered if he was much different.

Taylor lived with his Uncle Theo during the school year, partly because Uncle Theo lived so close to Thornhaven School, but mostly because his mother was too involved in her many social functions to bother with her son. As for Taylor's dad . . . well, as everyone liked to put it, Taylor's dad was "elsewhere."

That night after the first freeze tag game of the year, Uncle Theo dragged on his pipe and talked on and on without listening to a thing Taylor had to say.

"I remember seventh grade," he said wistfully, sitting in his recliner while Taylor hunched over the dining room table trying to make sense out of his homework. "That's when I first got on my school baseball team." Uncle Theo smiled and raised his eyebrows. "First took an interest in girls in seventh grade, too." He took a long drag on his pipe and spewed foul-smelling, sweet smoke into the heavy air.

"You play a sport?" Uncle Theo asked.

"Sort of," said Taylor, wondering if freeze tag qualified.

"Good. Sports are good for you. They teach you discipline. Give you a sense of accomplishment. Prepare you for life."

"But what if you never win?" asked Taylor. "What if winning is *impossible?*"

Uncle Theo waved his hand at the thought, and smoke flew through his fingers in cloudy puffs. "The answer to that is simple, my boy. You win. Period. The end." Then he sat up in his recliner and looked Taylor in the eye. "Our family is not a family of losers, Taylor. We have money because we win. We have respect because we win. We do not accept loss. Losing is not an option. Do you understand that?"

"Sure," said Taylor, hesitating. "I guess."

"Look at your father! He never gave up, and he became one of the most successful men in the state."

"Yeah, so how come he's in prison?" Taylor asked, defiantly.

Uncle Theo waved his hand again, as if it were a mere detail that didn't mean anything at all. "Your father's imprisonment does not change any of the things he accomplished."

Uncle Theo leaned closer. Taylor could smell the sickly aroma of ancient pipe ash on his smoking jacket. To Taylor it smelled like money. It smelled like success.

"The mind, my boy," he bellowed, pointing to his right temple. "It is the mind that makes all things possible. You'd be amazed if you knew all the things your mind is capable of. It can bring you riches. It can bring you power. It can bring your enemies crashing down like pillars of stone."

Taylor smiled at that. He liked that idea.

"You are a Sloat, Taylor. The power of your mind can move mountains. You could be every bit as successful as your father."

Taylor frowned at his uncle. "But . . . the things my father did . . ."

"Your father did only what was *necessary* to succeed," Uncle Theo said with a wave of his pipe. "He used his mind. He breathed sheer determination. I don't believe for an instant that he killed those investors."

Six lunch hours of freeze tag. Six more days without getting any closer to victory. Uncle Theo kept reminding Taylor that he was a Sloat, but he certainly didn't feel like one. Sloats never lost. Sloats always beat the odds. Sloats always emerged victorious. At home Taylor could barely face the family portraits lining the halls.

"What if I don't want to play anymore?" Taylor asked Mickey Van Horn on the seventh day of seventh grade. "I'm too old—we're *all* too old to play dumb old freeze tag."

Mickey just slammed his locker and laughed, his voice echoing in the empty stone hallway. "You'll never be too old for freeze tag, Taylor. You'll be playing freeze tag next year, and the year after. You'll be playing freeze tag for the rest of your life. You'll be an old man, on a cane, wheezing and coughing, and you'll still be chasing us. Because you'll still be *it.*"

"I'm not coming today," Taylor told Mickey, almost believing it himself.

Mickey just shook his head. "Oh, you'll be there," he said, so sure of himself it made Taylor sick. "You might not come today, and you might not come tomorrow, but you'll be there eventually. And we'll all be waiting for you."

Then Mickey turned on his heel and sauntered down the hall, his shoes clicking on the stone floor.

Taylor looked into his lunch bag, then hurled it into the trash. Any appetite he had was gone.

You'd be amazed at the things your mind is capable of . . . Uncle Theo's words sifted through Taylor's brain until it sounded like his uncle was right there next to him. Taylor tried to imagine the power his uncle and father must have had after amassing such great fortunes. What was it like to have so much money that every move you made affected the stock market, even affected the whole country? Those kinds of accomplishments seemed far beyond anything Taylor could imagine for himself.

But Uncle Theo was right. He was a Sloat, and maybe, just maybe, that counted for something.

Through the window at the end of the long hallway, Taylor could see kids pouring out of the heavy steel doors into the immense asphalt yard. Down by the far fence a few kids had already begun to gather.

The game was waiting for him. And Mickey was right, it would never end . . . not until Taylor won.

The wind scraped across the blacktop yard, sweeping dust and candy wrappers into the air, slamming them against the rusty chain-link fence. A cold front had moved in from the north, and the sun was nowhere to be seen. The kids playing in the yard exhaled puffs of rich steam. Ears and noses were already red, and it was just five minutes into lunch period.

Taylor Sloat crossed the dark asphalt, getting closer and closer to the mob of kids waiting for him against the back fence. Even then, as he approached, he felt a change— not just in the air around him, but in himself. Today was the last day he would ever need to play freeze tag. Losing would not be an option. Quitting would not be an option either. The only thing left was winning.

"You're late, Sloat," said Mickey Van Horn, acting as if he knew all along that Taylor would show up.

"Shut up and play," said Taylor. He held out his hands and balanced on the balls of his feet, waiting for kids to start jumping away from the fence. He was ready.

As always, Mickey started the game by being the first off the fence. Taylor leapt at him and missed. Mickey laughed and taunted him. This was okay. Taylor had plenty of time to catch Mickey. For now, Taylor settled on the kids who weren't so fast. For the first time since third grade, he felt in control of the game. Fat Eddie froze first, then Cody. One by one, Taylor forced them to freeze in their tracks, and for once he was freezing them faster than they were being defrosted.

Mickey was getting mad. He began to shout orders at people, screaming at kids who left the fence without being told.

Once they tried to form a chain from the fence, all of them holding hands and reaching out to unfreeze the others, but their hands slipped and Taylor raced into the mob of kids as they tried to run back to safety, tagging them all until there were only three kids to freeze.

There were still fifteen minutes left to lunch, and against all odds, Taylor knew that today he would win the game. Then something happened.

Fat Eddie thawed.

No one tagged him. No one even came close to tagging him—he just spontaneously defrosted.

"No fair!" Taylor screamed at Fat Eddie, who was racing back to the fence. "You were frozen!"

"Was not," said Fat Eddie. "I was just pretending." And he began to go around unfreezing other kids.

Taylor tried to shout his protests, but it didn't matter. Soon other kids unfroze themselves the moment Taylor's back was turned.

"Cheaters!" screamed Taylor. "You're all cheating!"

"I don't think so," said Mickey, as he ran around Taylor with a big smile on his face. "Hey, guys, is anyone cheating?"

"No!" they all shouted.

Mickey shrugged. "Majority rules."

And in less than a minute, two dozen kids were buzzing around Taylor like a swarm of gnats—not a single one of them frozen.

Taylor clenched his fists and felt his hands go cold—*very* cold. His knuckles turned white. There were still ten minutes left to the lunch period.

He opened his palms and looked at his hands. He focused all his anger toward the tips of his fingers, and felt a sense of icy determination fill his body. It ran up from his toes, through his legs, through his arms, and finally it surged into his fingertips.

Losing is not an option, his mind chanted. *Losing is not an option.*

He looked at the kids swarming and laughing around him, and returned all his attention to the game.

"Can't get me!" shouted Fat Eddie, looming in orbit around him like a slow-moving planet.

Taylor grabbed his arm, gripping it tightly. "Wanna bet?" Suddenly Fat Eddie froze. He didn't just stop moving, he *froze*. His eyes locked in place; his jaw stopped moving. Taylor could feel the fat in Eddie's arm becoming hard as stone as his blood turned to ice. He quickly let go. Fat Eddie was nothing more than an ice statue encased in human flesh.

But no one noticed—they were too busy buzzing around Taylor in the frenzy of the game.

So Taylor tagged another, and another. Freezing

them in their tracks. It wasn't until Mickey and some of the others raced off the fence to defrost their friends that they realized something was terribly wrong—the frozen kids would not thaw.

"What's going on?" shouted Mickey. He looked into Greasy Cody's eyes. "Hey, Cody?" Cody didn't blink. Mickey reached out and touched Cody's eyeball, which was frozen solid. Mickey opened his mouth to scream, but nothing came out.

"New rules," said Taylor. "My rules."

Taylor slapped Rex McMillan on the back. Rex skidded for a few feet and came to rest, frozen in the middle of a stride.

Taylor weaved in and out of the frozen kids, tagging those who were still free. A few tried to get away, but no one did. One or two screamed, but the teachers were used to kids screaming in the yard—especially back by the freeze tag corner—and they paid no attention.

At last, everyone was frozen—everyone except Mickey Van Horn.

Mickey hid behind Fat Eddie, and when Taylor spotted him, Mickey made a mad dash for the fence. Taylor leaped at him, but Mickey crashed into the fence, getting his hands and clothes covered with ancient rust.

Taylor stood inches away, hands out, balancing on the balls of his feet, guarding Mickey like a cat. Mickey clutched the fence for dear life. It was his base, his lifeline, and they both knew the second he took his hand off that fence, he was history.

"Okay, okay, Taylor," said Mickey, gripping the fence so tightly his fingers were starting to bleed. "You win!

Game's over."

Taylor shook his head. "Uh-uh. No quitting. I don't win until everyone's frozen. That's the rule."

Mickey looked at the human sculpture garden around him.

"I don't wanna play," Mickey whined, sounding like the third grader he had been when the game began all those years ago. "You can't make me."

But Taylor just smiled.

"The bell will ring," said Mickey, looking at his watch. "In one minute the bell will ring, and if you tag me it won't count. I won't be frozen."

Taylor knew that this was true—if Mickey held on to the fence long enough, the game would have to be continued tomorrow, and who knew what tricks Mickey would have up his sleeve by then. So Taylor bluffed.

"The bell won't ring," he said. "It won't ring, because *I* won't let it ring."

There was no truth to this, but there must have been something about the look in Taylor's eyes, because Mickey believed it. He screamed and made a mad dash for the school.

Taylor reached for him.

Mickey leaped into the air.

Taylor tagged him . . .

And the bell rang.

But it rang one moment too late for Mickey.

He crystallized from the point where Taylor touched him and all throughout his body. Taylor watched as Mickey sailed through the air. Then, his icy body fell to the asphalt. As it did, Mickey Van Horn shattered into a thousand pieces, like a bag of ice dropped from a roof.

The largest piece of Mickey Van Horn bounced away, rolling toward the teachers at the far end of the yard. In a moment, they began to scream and came racing to the spot where Taylor stood among the other frozen boys.

But this was all right. After all, it was just a game—and the game, as Uncle Theo had said, prepared Taylor for life. He had won and had finally proved himself a Sloat. His father would be proud.

CAR FOUR

IT BEGAN WHEN THEY REDECORATED MY FATHER'S OFFICE
building. The lobby used to be warm and friendly, with a big
vase of dried flowers on an oak table surrounded by soft,
comfortable chairs. When they redecorated, all this was
replaced by stiff, black leather chairs and an ugly chrome
table. The walls were now unpainted concrete, as if the
building were still under construction, and icy blue lights
threw patterns of shadow on the wall. It all looked very
trendy, but to me it just felt cold. *Who would want to work
here?* I thought, wishing things didn't always have to change.

My brother and I both got the chills as we walked
into that stark, unpleasant lobby. Markie grabbed my hand
tightly as we stepped up to the security guard.

"Marissa, this isn't Dad's building," said Markie.

"Don't be dumb. Of course it is," I said like a stern
older sister.

Even the security guard was new—a pale-looking
man with sunken cheeks, and eyes the same color as the
concrete walls. Behind him a giant, gunmetal-gray clock

that looked like a gear in some terrible factory sliced the hour into minutes with steely hands as sharp as knives. The grim guard stared at us coldly, as if we were trespassing on a grave.

"May I help you?" he asked.

I sighed and went through the speech as quickly as possible. "We're Markie and Marissa Hernandez. Our father is Carlos Hernandez, of Hernandez and Stevens, Attorneys at Law. Our mom *always* drops us off every Friday at five so we can spend the weekend with our father."

"They're divorced," said Markie, whispering it like it was a big terrible disease.

The gloomy guard nodded and sent us on our way. We headed toward the elevator banks, our sneakers squeaking on the gray marble floor.

Even the elevators had changed; the wood-paneled doors were now shiny, mirrored steel.

As we approached the elevator bank, Markie clutched his stuffed elephant to his chest and took a deep breath, a routine he repeated whenever we got near an elevator.

I guess most kids love elevators, especially fast ones that make you feel heavy on the way up and tingly light on the way down. Not Markie, though. Markie hates elevators.

When he was four we were in an elevator at the mall—a stupid elevator, really, since the mall only had two floors and the elevator moved so slowly you could climb the stairs faster. Still, Markie and I wanted to ride the elevator, so Mom, Dad, Markie, and I got in. But just as the door was closing, Markie saw that he had dropped his teddy bear just outside of the elevator car. As he grabbed it, the door closed on his hand and slowly began to rise to the second floor.

It was awful. Mom began to scream, and both she and Dad, in a panic, fought to pry the elevator doors open. But they wouldn't budge. Markie began to howl as my parents started tugging on his arm. They were looking at his arm, but I was looking at his eyes, and I knew the moment it happened. It was the moment his pupils went wide. He gasped, and in that second, his face became mottled purple and red, and he screamed like I never heard anyone scream before.

Finally, after what seemed like an eternity, the elevator reached the second floor. The bell dinged cheerfully, and the doors pulled apart as if nothing had happened.

The people waiting outside the elevator were the first to see it. They saw a screaming boy gripping the severed leg of a teddy bear, his own bloody hand missing a pinky.

Mom and Dad blamed each other for that and lots of other things, and eventually got divorced. Dad, being a hotshot lawyer, filed a lawsuit against the mall and won enough money to put Markie and me through college someday. I never knew a pinky could be worth so much money.

The accident was three years ago, but to Markie it might as well have been yesterday.

Now he clutched the stuffed elephant that had replaced his ruined teddy bear, practically strangling the thing as we approached the new mirrored doors of the elevator bank in Dad's office building. Markie walked slowly and fearfully, just as he had when we went to Nana's funeral last year.

Three of the four elevators were out of service, leaving only one car—car four—to carry people to the building's thirty floors.

"Mechanical problems," I said, reading the sign for Markie.

"What kind of mechanical problems?" he asked.

I considered making up a story about how someone was cut in half, but decided against it. "They probably just need to grease the gears or something," I told him.

Finally car four arrived, and a wave of people flowed out like sardines from a can, and smelling just as bad. When the car was empty, people forced their way in ahead of us, and Markie and I barely squeezed into the car.

The inside of the elevator used to be paneled wood, but now the walls and ceiling were mirrored glass, making the small, crowded elevator seem like an immense hall packed with a thousand people trapped deep within the glass. The mirrored walls reflected each other over and over, sending light ping-ponging back and forth in the little box of a room, like a fun house where no one was having fun.

The elevator door slammed behind Markie, and as the elevator rose, my ears began to pop. That's when I noticed that Markie, standing with his back up against the door, was sobbing silently to himself.

"Markie, are you okay?"

"It's eating me," he whispered through his tears.

"What?"

"The elevator is eating me." He was terrified, and his face was turning that awful shade of purple. When I looked behind him, I saw that the right cheek of his behind was firmly pinched between the steel elevator doors.

"Help me," he whimpered.

Other people began to notice and tried to help, but the doors would not open a fraction of an inch. Markie sobbed until the door finally opened, and car four released him from its steel jaws.

Once we were in Dad's office, it took half an hour to calm Markie down. Dad examined his rear to find a thin red welt, as if Markie had been pinched in a vise. To make things worse, somewhere between the first and twenty-third floors Markie had managed to lose his little stuffed elephant. He swore that the elevator ate it.

On the way down to the lobby, Dad had to hold Markie in his arms. Markie clung to him, holding his breath and squeezing his eyes shut.

There were just the three of us in the elevator, and I quickly realized how terrible car four truly was. With nothing but mirrors everywhere, all I could see was a thousand reflections of us stretching in all directions toward a dim, gray infinity. All I could hear was the wind whistling in the shaft. All I could smell was an awful aroma of the new gray carpet beneath my feet. I have to admit, I closed my eyes and began to hold my breath long before we reached the lobby.

The following Friday, Mom dropped us off at the steps of Dad's office building as she always did.

"Can't you come up with us?" begged Markie.

"It's not a good idea," said Mom, which was her nice way of saying that she never wanted to see Dad again for as long as she lived.

"Please . . ." Markie pleaded.

"Markie," said Mom, "it only takes you a minute to get to his office."

"A minute is a long way," said Markie.

Mom unfastened his seatbelt for him and stuffed a brand-new teddy bear into his arms. "It's okay, honey," she said. "Marissa will protect you."

I hated her for that.

We climbed the steps toward the tower, nearing the revolving doors that spun like propellers, sucking people in and spitting people out.

"Sometimes," said Markie, "sometimes I'm afraid I'll get lost between Mom and Dad."

"Don't be silly," I told him, but I knew exactly how he felt. It was like last year when I flew out alone to visit Aunt Lita. There's no lonelier moment in the universe than the moment between your family and the plane. There's a long hallway you have to go through after you've said good-bye to your mom before the stewardess finally greets you at the plane's hatch. That hallway has to be the longest, most awful hallway in the world—and that's how the trip from Mom's car to Dad's office must have felt to Markie.

Together we let ourselves be sucked into the revolving doors and spat out into the bleak lobby.

We waited in silence at the elevator banks. All four elevators were working, but car four was the first one to arrive.

"No!" Markie held me back, so we waited for the next elevator. Car four came back before any of the others.

Markie stood back and we waited once more. Two minutes passed, and at last an elevator came. Car four, again.

This time I felt so stupid about it that I made Markie get into the crowded elevator, figuring all the others were just tied up on high floors. I pushed Markie in first, making sure I was between him and the closing doors.

Then the elevator started to move.

Down.

Markie gasped, and so did I. I know this is dumb, but

there's something truly terrifying about getting in an elevator and feeling it go in the wrong direction. Sure, what goes down has to come back up, but for that tiny split second before your brain makes sense of what's going on, all you can feel is the sudden panic that something's gone wrong. Even when your brain kicks in a moment later, some of that feeling stays with you.

The elevator emptied out on the underground parking levels, leaving Markie and me to ride up alone. With the elevator empty, Markie pushed himself up against the back wall, as far away from the doors as he could get. He plastered himself against the mirrored wall, gripping his new teddy bear, which didn't seem to give him any of the comfort his little stuffed elephant had given him.

Marissa will protect you. Mom's words rang in my ears. I wished she had never given that responsibility to me.

I pushed 23—Dad's floor—and watched as the numbers began to climb. My ears started to pop and I tried to avoid looking at the thousand reflections of myself in the mirrors around me. No one else got in.

"See, Markie?" I said, turning to him. "There's nothing to worry about . . ." That's when I realized that I wasn't looking at Markie at all; I was looking at one of his reflections in the mirror. I turned to look the other way.

"Markie?"

I reached to touch him, but my hand fell upon cold glass.

I spun around. Markie was nowhere . . . and everywhere! There were a hundred reflections of him, but that's all they were—*reflections*. I reached to all the walls, desperately touching them with my fingertips, but Markie was not

107

in the elevator! It was as if he had somehow slipped into the mirrors and was lost somewhere *inside* them.

"Marissa?" Markie began to move, and his thousand reflections shifted like a human kaleidoscope. I could see him in the mirrors, reaching toward my reflections, trying to find the real me, the same way I was trying to find the real him. He began to cry. "Marissa, where are you?" He turned and headed deeper into the maze of reflections, getting farther and farther away.

"Marissa?!" he screamed, panicking now, trapped. I saw his many reflections run deeper into the mirrors, getting smaller and smaller.

"Marissa!" he screamed more frantically. "Where are

you? Don't leave me all alone!"

"Markie!" I screamed back. "No!" But he couldn't hear me anymore. All I could do was scream and press my hands against the cold glass, watching as my little brother went deeper and deeper into the mirrors—until he was just a shadow that disappeared into the dark distance. Soon, his voice faded into the whistling wind racing through the elevator shaft, and there was nothing left around me but my own reflections, stretching in all directions forever and ever and ever.

The bell dinged cheerfully and the elevator door opened.

"Marissa?" It was my father, who must have heard me screaming. In tears I raced out of the elevator into his arms.

"Honey, what's wrong? Where's Markie?"

"He's gone, Daddy," I wailed. "Markie's gone!"

"What do you mean, *gone?*"

And then my dad noticed something that I didn't. Lying there in the corner of the elevator was Markie's stuffed elephant, the one that had vanished in the elevator the week before.

"Markie?" Just as Dad reached into the elevator, the door closed on his arm, all the way up to his shoulder.

"Daddy, no!" I shrieked.

People yelled and tried to pry him free, but all I could do was watch my father's eyes as car four began its return trip to the lobby.

RESTING DEEP

My parents dropped me off at his house late last night.

Greaty's house.

That's what I call him, "Greaty"—short for Great-grandpa. He's the oldest in the family. He's buried two wives, two sons, and one daughter.

His house is small: a living room, a bedroom, and a tiny kitchen. It's really a shack in a row of other shacks, where ancient people cling to their last days.

It smells old here. It smells salty, like the sea. And Greaty's always eating the fish he catches.

"Good to see you, Tommy," he said to me at the door, smiling his long-toothed smile.

Whenever I see his smile, I run my tongue along my braces, feeling the crooked contour of my own teeth, wondering if one day mine will look like his, all yellow and twisted.

"Ready for a good day of fishing tomorrow?" he asked.

"Sure, I guess."

My parents left me here to spend a night and a day.

They do this every year, four times a year. It started when I was little. It had to do with my fear of water. Mom and Dad decided that the best way for me to get over it was to send me out with Greaty on his big fishing boat. Then I'd see how much fun water could be.

But it didn't work that way.

Greaty would always tell tales of sharks and whales and mermaids who dragged fishermen down to their watery graves. Going out with him made me more afraid of the water than I had been before, so afraid that I never learned to swim. Still, I went out with him and continue to go. It's become a family tradition. Sometimes, I'm ashamed to say, I hope for the day when Greaty joins his two wives, two sons, and one daughter, so I don't have to go out to sea with him ever again.

It is an hour before dawn now. Greaty and I always set out when everything is cold, dark, and still, and my veins feel full of ice water. I watch him as he prepares his boat. It's an old fishing boat, its wooden hull marred with gouges from years of banging up against the dock. When a wave rides it high against its berth, I can see the barnacles crusted on its belly. It has been years since Greaty has bothered to have them scraped off.

He calls his boat the *Mariana*, "named after the deepest trench in the ocean," he once told me. "That trench is seven miles deep, and it's where the great mysteries of the world still lie undiscovered."

I sometimes think about the trench. I think about all the ships and planes that have fallen down there in wars. I imagine being in a ship that had seven miles to sink before hitting bottom. That's like falling from space.

We set out, and by the time dawn arrives, we are already far from shore. I can tell that the day is not going to be a pleasant one. The sun is hidden behind clouds. There is a storm to the north, and it's churning up the waves.

Greaty heads due north into the choppy waves. He stares at the horizon and occasionally says something to me just to let me know he hasn't forgotten me.

"Today's going to be an exceptional day," he tells me. "One day in a million. I can feel it in my bones."

I can feel it in my bones, too, but not what Greaty feels. I feel a miserable sense of dread creaking through all of my joints. Something is going to happen today—I know it, and it is not something good. I imagine giant tidal waves looming over us, swallowing us in cold waters and sending us down to the very bottom, where it is so dark the fish don't have eyes.

Half an hour later, the shore behind us is just a thin line of gray on the horizon. Greaty has never taken me out this far before. Never.

"Maybe we'd better stop here," I tell him. "We're getting kind of far from shore."

"We'll stop soon," he says. "We're almost there."

Almost where? I wonder. But Greaty doesn't say anything more about it. His silence is strange. I don't know what he's thinking—I never do.

And then something suddenly strikes me in a way that it has never struck me before—I don't know my great-grandfather. I've spent days and weekends with him every few months for my entire life, but I don't *know* him. I don't know what he thinks and what he feels. All I know about him is the way he baits his hooks, the way he talks about fishing. I can't get the feeling out of my head that suddenly I'm out on a boat with a stranger.

"You know how many great-grandchildren I have, Tommy?" he asks, shoving a wad of chewing tobacco into the corner of his mouth. "Twelve."

"That's a lot," I say with a nervous chuckle.

"You know how many of them I take fishing with me?" He stares at me, chewing up and down, with a smile on his crooked, tobacco-filled mouth.

"Just me?"

He points his gnarled bony finger at me.

"Just you."

He waits for me to ask the obvious question, but I don't.

"You want to know why I take only you?" he asks. "Well, I'll tell you. There's your cousins, the Sloats. With all the money they've got, they can buy their kids anything in the world. Those kids are set for life. Then there's your other cousins, the Tinkertons. They've got brains coming out of them like sweat. They'll all amount to something. And your Aunt Rebecca's kids—they're beautiful. All that golden hair—they'll get by on their looks."

"So?" I ask.

"So," he says. "What about you?"

What about me? I take after my mother—skinny as a rail, a bit of an overbite. And I got my father's big ears, too. Okay, so I'm not the best-looking kid. As for money, we live in a small, crummy house, and we probably won't ever afford anything better. As for brains, I'm a C student. Always have been.

The old man sees me mulling myself over. "*Now* do you know?" he asks.

I can't look at Greaty. I can only look down, feeling inadequate and ashamed. "Because I'm ugly . . . because I'm poor . . . because I'm stupid?"

Greaty laughs at that, showing his big teeth. I never realized how far the gums had receded away from them, like a wave recedes from the shore. He should have had all his teeth pulled out and replaced by fake ones. The way they are now, they're awful, like teeth in a skull.

"I picked you because you were the special one, Tommy," he says. "You were the one *without* all the things the others have. To me that makes you special."

He turns the wheel and heads toward the dark storm clouds on the horizon.

"I was like you, Tommy," he tells me. "So you're the one I want to take with me."

The waves begin to get rough, rolling up and down like tall black hills and deep, dark valleys. The wind breathes past us, moaning like a living thing, and I feel seasickness begin to take hold in my gut.

Greaty must see me starting to turn green.

"How afraid of the water are you, Tommy?" he asks.

"About as afraid as a person can get," I tell him.

"You know," he says, "the ocean's not a bad place. When I die, I would like to die in the ocean." He paused. "I think I will."

I swallow hard. I don't like it when Greaty talks about dying. He does it every once in a while. It's like he sees the world around him changing—the neighborhood being torn down to build condos, the marshes paved over for supermarkets. He knows that he'll be torn off this world soon, too, so he talks about it, as if talking about it will make it easier when the time comes.

"Why are we heading into the storm?" I ask Greaty.

He doesn't say anything for a long time.

"Don't you worry about that," he finally says coldly. "A man can catch his best fish on the edge of a storm."

We travel twenty minutes more, and as we go I peer over the side, where I see fins—dorsal fins, sticking out of the water—and I'm terrified.

"Dolphins," says Greaty, as if reading the fear in my face.

Sure enough, he is right. Dolphins are riding along with the boat. As I look into the distance, I see dozens of them, all running in line with us, as if it is a race. And then suddenly they stop.

I go to the stern of the boat and look behind us. The dolphins are still there, but they wait far behind. The bottle-tips of their noses poke out of the water, forming a line a hundred yards away, like a barrier marking off one part of the ocean from the other.

I look down at the waters we've come into and could swear that, as black as the waters were before, they're even blacker now. And the smell of the sea has changed, too.

Greaty stops the boat.

"We're here," he tells me.

He gets out his fishing rod, and one for me. Then he

pulls out bait, impaling the small feeder fish onto tiny barbed hooks.

Suddenly, the boat pitches with a wave. It goes up and down like an elevator—like a wild ride at an amusement park. My stomach hangs in midair and then falls down to my toes.

The water rises around the boat, almost flowing in, but the boat rises with it.

"You know why a boat floats?" he asks me.

"Why does a boat float, Greaty?"

"Because it's too afraid of what's under the water," he says, completely serious.

Greaty throws his line in, and we wait, he sitting there calmly, and I, shivering, with sweaty palms. I watch lightning strike in the far, far distance.

Greaty knows what he's doing, I tell myself. *He's been fishing his whole life. He knows how close you can get to a storm and still be safe . . . doesn't he?*

I haven't thrown my line in yet. It's as if throwing a line into the water brings me closer to it, and I don't want to be closer to it. I watch my feeder fish, sewed onto the steel hook, writhe in silent agony until it finally goes limp. Greaty watches the fish die.

"Dying is the natural course of things, you know," he says. "Bad thing about dying, though, is having to die alone. I don't want to die alone." Then he turns to me and says, "When I go, I want somebody to come with me."

He takes my line, casts it into the water, and hands me back the rod. I feel the line being pulled away from the boat as the hook sinks deeper and deeper. Lightning flashes on the distant horizon.

"The person who dies with me, though, ought to be someone I care about. Someone *special,*" he says.

"I gotta use the bathroom," I tell him, even though I don't have to. I just have to get away, as far away as I can. I have to go where I don't see the ocean, or the storm, or Greaty.

I go down to the cabin, and there I feel something cold on my feet. I look down and see water.

I race back up top. "Greaty," I say. "There's water down below! We're leaking."

But he isn't bothered. He just holds his line and chews his tobacco. "Guess old *Mariana* decided she's not so afraid of the ocean after all."

"We gotta start bailing! We have to do something!"

"Don't you worry, Tommy," he tells me in a soft, calm voice. "She takes on a little water now and then. It doesn't mean anything."

"Are you sure?"

"Of course I'm sure."

Then Greaty's line goes taut, and his pole begins to bend. He skillfully fights the fish on the other end, letting out some line, then pulling some in—out, in, out, in, until the fish on the other end is exhausted.

In the distance behind us, the dolphins watch.

I hear the snagged fish thump against the boat, and Greaty, his old muscles straining, reels it in.

At first I'm not sure what I'm seeing, and then it becomes clear. The thing on the end of the line is like no fish I've ever laid eyes on. It is ugly and gray, covered with slime rather than scales. It has a long neck like a baby giraffe, and its head is filled with teeth. It has only one eye, in the center of its forehead—a clouded, unseeing eye.

Greaty drops the thing onto the deck, and it flops around, making an awful growling, hissing noise. Its head flies to the left and then to the right on the end of its long neck, until finally it collapses.

Greaty looks at it long and hard. Far behind us, the dolphins wait at the edge of the black waters.

"What is it, Greaty?"

"It doesn't have a name, Tommy," he tells me, as he heads into his tackle room. "It doesn't have a name."

He comes out of the boat with a new fishing rod—a heavy pole, with heavy line and a hook the size of a meat hook. He digs the hook into the thing he caught and hurls it back into the ocean, letting it pull out far into the dark waters.

What could he possibly be trying to catch with something that large?

"Greaty, I want to go home now." I can hear the distant rumble of thunder. The storm coming toward us is as black as the sea. When I look down into the cabin, the water level has risen. There is at least a foot of water down there, and the boat is leaning horribly to starboard.

"Greaty!" I scream. "Are you listening to me?"

"We're not going home, Tommy."

I hear what he's saying, but I can't believe it. "What?" I shout at him. "What did you say?"

"Don't you see, Tommy?" he tells me. "There are places out here—wondrous places that no one has ever charted. Places deeper than the Mariana Trench, bottomless places where creatures dwell that no man has ever seen."

The boat pitches terribly. Water pours in from the side.

"We're going to be part of that mystery, Tommy, you and me, together. We're going to rest deep."

"No!" I scream. "You can't do this! I don't want to die out here!"

"Tommy, you're not doing anyone else on this earth any good," he explains to me. "You won't be missed by many, and even then you won't be missed for long. I'm the only one who needs you, Tommy. So I won't be alone."

"I won't do it!"

Greaty laughs. "Well, seeing as how the boat is sinking and a storm's coming, it doesn't look like you have much of a choice. Not unless you can walk on water!"

A wave lifts the boat high and water pours in, filling the cabin. And then something tugs on Greaty's line so hard that it pulls the rod right out of his hand. It disappears into the water.

"I think it's time," he says.

I scramble into the flooding cabin and find a life jacket. I put it on, as if it can really help me.

When I come out, the water gets calm, and I feel something scraping along the bottom of the boat—something huge.

I look up to the sky, wishing that I could sprout wings and fly away from the sea. Then something rises out of the water in front of us—a big, slimy black fin the size of a great sail, and beneath that fin, two humps on a creature's back—a creature larger than any whale could possibly be.

"Look at that!" shouts Greaty.

The fin crosses before us, towering over our heads, and then submerges, disappearing into the black depths.

It gets very quiet, much too quiet. Greaty puts his hand on my shoulder.

"Thank you," he whispers. "Thank you, Tommy, for

coming with me."

Somewhere below, I hear a rush of water as something coming from very, very deep forces its way toward the surface, getting closer and closer. The water around us begins to bubble and churn.

"No!" I scream, and climb up to the edge of the sinking boat.

I never thought that I would leap into the ocean by choice, but that's exactly what I do. My feet leave the gouged old wood of the *Mariana*, and in a moment I am underwater.

The water is icy cold all around me, salty and rough. I break surface, and gasp for air. My life jacket is all that keeps me from sinking into this bottomless ocean pit. A wave washes me away from the boat.

Then I hear a roar and the cracking of wood. A great gush of water catches me in the eyes, making them sting. I turn back, and see it only for an instant. Something huge, black, and covered with ooze. It has sharp teeth and no eyes, and a black, forked tongue that has forced its way through the hull of the boat, searching for Greaty like a tentacle . . . and finding him. The thing crushes the entire boat in its immense jaws. Its roar is so loud, I cannot hear if Greaty is screaming.

A wave hits, and I am under the water again. When I break surface, the beast, the boat, and Greaty are gone. Only churning water and bubbles remain where they had been.

Far away, I can see the dolphins waiting at the edge of this unholy water. I move my arms and kick my legs, teaching myself to swim.

I will not join you in your bottomless grave, Greaty. I

will not let you take me with you. You will be alone. And even though I am out in the middle of the ocean at the edge of a storm, I will not die this way. I will not.

Something huge and smooth brushes past my feet, but I don't think about it. Something rough and hard scrapes against my leg, but I only look forward, staring at the dolphins lined up a hundred yards away. Those dolphins are waiting for me, I know. They will not dare come into these waters, but if I make it back to them, I know that I will be all right. They will carry me home.

And so I will ignore the horrors that swarm unseen beneath me. I will close my ears to the roars and groans from the awful deep. And I will get to the dolphins, even if I have to walk on water.

SHADOWS OF DOUBT

In the blink of an eye, you might suddenly feel
That your world's been invaded by all things unreal.
They slink up behind you, and don't make a sound,
But there's nothing to fear . . . if you don't turn around.

In the pit of your stomach there rests a device
That can calculate how fast your blood turns to ice;
It measures the temperature nightmares will start,
Then divides it by beats of a terrified heart.

At the foot of your bed lies a blanket of fear,
You might think it's quite safe, but it's always quite near.
When its steel-woolen quilting wraps 'round you one night,
You may learn that it's not only bedbugs that bite.

At the top of the stairs there's an attic I've found,
That remained even after the house was torn down,
And it's filled with the cobwebs of lonely old dreams,
Which have grown into nightmares that swing from the beams.

DARKNESS CREEPING

At the mouth of a cave lives a shadow of doubt,
If you dare to go in, will you ever come out?
Are there creatures who lurk where it's too dim to see?
Can you hear when they move? Are you scared yet? (Who, me?)

At the edge of the earth flows a river of fear,
And it pours into space day by day, year by year.
As you shoot the cold rapids, and stray far from shore,
Do you notice your lifeboat has just lost an oar?

In the eye of the storm stands a ghost of a chance,
And around her all spirits are destined to dance.
She turns a cold gaze toward an unlucky few—
Don't dare to look now, for she's staring at you.

At the end of the world stands a giant steel door,
And what lies beyond it, nobody's quite sure . . .
Is it crystal-clear heavens, or night blazing hot,
And which is more frightening: knowing, or not?

In the face of the future we fly on our own,
Hoping our wings never turn into stone.
If you fall from that sky to the sea, will you drown?
Well, there's no need to worry . . . unless you look down.

At the back of your mind, there's a hole open wide,
Where the darkness is creeping in from the outside,
You can light rows of candles to cast the dark out,
But it's always there hiding . . .

                              . . . in shadows of doubt.